COLD REVENGE

A MEGAN SCOTT / MICHAEL ELLIOTT MYSTERY

SANDRA NIKOLAI

COLD REVENGE

Copyright © 2019 by Sandra Nikolai

www.sandranikolai.com

Vemcort Publishing

ISBN: 978-1-989011-04-1 (ebook)

ISBN: 978-1-989011-06-5 (paperback)

ISBN: 978-1-989011-13-3 (audiobook)

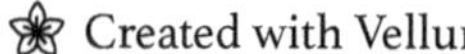 Created with Vellum

*To my readers, thank you for allowing me
to be a part of your lives.*

1

———

MEGAN

Tuesday morning, September 25

The century-year-old home on St. Catherine Street West had more character than a troupe of Shakespearian actors, but it also came with a lot of baggage. Michael and I couldn't begin to afford the repairs it required, despite the real estate agent's efforts this morning to negotiate a better price for us.

Michael unlocked the door to our condo. "Brett has one more two-story house to show us tonight," he said, referring to Brett Paquette, our agent with the Montreal-Res Group, or MRG. "It's on Hillside Avenue in the same upscale neighborhood as the others."

Only a ten-minute drive away. And yet... "I can't go with you tonight," I said, removing my coat and hanging it in the hall closet. "I have a meeting with a client."

"No problem." He shrugged out of his leather jacket. "I'll go to the showing alone. Brett told me the house is a more recent construction. He said it's perfect for us. If he's right, I'll book a second visit so we can go see it together."

"Brett said the two older homes we visited this week would be perfect for us too, and we didn't like either one. That's not counting the others we visited over the last months." I sighed in exasperation.

Michael frowned. "We can't afford to be picky, Megan. Not many homes come up for sale in this area. Most have stayed in the family for decades." He headed for the living room and draped his jacket over the leather sofa bordering the window.

"But these houses are so expensive," I protested, sitting down next to him on the sofa. "I can't even imagine how we'd be able to afford a million-dollar house."

"Don't worry. Like I told you before, I'll use the inheritance funds from my grandmother to help with the down payment."

"Are you sure you want to do that?"

"Yes. What else could be more important than buying the house we love?"

"What about your parents? What will they say?"

He smiled. "Are you kidding? They'll be glad to hear I'm finally putting my grandmother's money to good use. To be clear, I still refuse to take a penny from my parents."

It was the first time Michael had mentioned his family in a while, albeit with a hint of irony. He was willing to withdraw funds from his grandmother's inheritance fund but accepting money from his parents was taboo.

And all because of a silly feud that began years ago. Michael had refused his father's offer to run his profitable high-tech company. He chose a career path as a crime reporter instead. To make matters worse, he rejected his parents' lavish lifestyle and the trust fund that came with it.

Although he hadn't admitted as much, the chill in his relationship with his father had created a void in his life that he attempted to fill with investigative assignments. But work was no replacement for family.

"I don't especially like living in old houses," I said, picking up our conversation, "but I love the area. I feel safe here. As long as we can furnish and decorate our home the way we want, I'm okay with it."

"We both like modern furniture combined with the odd vintage piece," Michael said, "so I don't see a problem. Once we get settled in our new home, we can make all sorts of plans... like getting married, raising a family—"

"Aren't you rushing things a little? We haven't even found the right house yet."

He grew pensive. "This isn't about the house, is it? You just don't trust me enough to marry me. Say it."

"I trust you, Michael," I said.

"Then we can talk about our future together, can't we?"

I loved Michael and considered myself the luckiest woman in the world to have such a caring man in my life, but I had no intention of encouraging a conversation about marriage right now. I'd survived a first failed marriage and a murdered husband. Living with Michael, and the next step of buying a house together, suited me fine.

I diverted the subject. "Speaking of family, we should visit your parents one day."

He eyed me with caution. "Why?"

"Why not?"

He glanced away.

His silence offended me. "I've only met them a few times. And we haven't seen them since they left Montreal and moved to their new home in the countryside a year ago."

"What's the rush?"

So it wasn't about me after all. "You don't have to keep proving yourself to your father, Michael."

"I'm not."

"Really? Raising the bar with each new investigative assignment you take on. Ensuring the risks get riskier."

"Taking risks comes with a crime reporter's job. We've been through this before." He raised his hands and let them fall to his lap with a thud.

His words brought back the memory of a confrontation he'd once had with a knife-wielding drug trafficker. The tiny scar on his cheek was a memento of how he'd managed to fight him off and survive the ordeal.

"Why are we having this discussion in the first place?" Michael stood up.

"It's about family," I said. "You've met several of my relatives, and my mother invites us over often. When will we see your parents again?"

"I don't know. I've been busy."

I shook my head in frustration. "You're always busy."

His cell phone rang. He checked the display and grimaced.

"What is it?" I asked.

"Nothing...just a message. I have a meeting at *The Gazette* this morning. I'd better go. I'll call you later." He gave me a quick kiss, grabbed his jacket, and briskly walked out the door, taking our unresolved issues with him.

Twenty steps down the hallway took me to my home office —one of the advantages that working as a freelance ghostwriter for Bradford Publishing offered. Although I enjoyed meeting with the staff and clients there on occasion, I appreciated the anonymity of working behind the scenes. The security of my home and the predictability of the job schedule appealed to me most of all.

Unlike Michael's job. His work called for intuitive thinking in the pursuit of justice. Meeting informants in the shadows of night. Accompanying the police on drug raids. It was risky and unpredictable.

A sudden regret washed over me. I wished I could take back the words I'd said to him moments ago. It wasn't my place to fault him for being a risk-taker. He loved his job. Exposing criminals of all stripes and their crimes boosted his confidence in his efforts. He'd won journalism awards and written a successful crime novel—tangible proof that his heart was in his work.

But according to Michael, he hadn't attained his desired level of worthiness. It was a higher goal he insisted on achieving before he rekindled long lost ties with his parents. It meant consistently seeking out more dangerous assignments to prove his success to them.

My greatest fear was that, one day, he might just take one risk too many.

And I didn't want to lose him.

2

———

MEGAN

Tuesday afternoon

I changed into a white shirt and matching navy-blue jacket and pants, then drove downtown to Bradford Publishing later in the afternoon to drop off a project. I could have sent it to Kayla by email, but I liked to show my face there from time to time. It gave me visibility as a working professional, as well as an occasion to ask about upcoming ghostwriting projects.

Kayla greeted me in the reception area, her height towering above me despite my three-inch heels. She smiled as she accepted my flash drive. "Thanks, Megan. By the way, how's that author's biography coming along?"

"I'm meeting with the client here tonight to tie up the loose ends," I said. "I should have it completed by the end of the week."

"Today's Tuesday. By Friday afternoon at five o'clock then?" As Bradford's project manager, Kayla was a stickler for details.

"Sure," I said. "Any other projects I can help you with?"

"Nothing right now. As soon as something comes in, I'll let you know."

"Thanks, Kayla."

I took the elevator back down. My phone rang as I was leaving the building. It was Michael.

"Megan, something's come up." He sounded disheartened. "I won't be able to go to the house showing tonight. I'm meeting an informant across town. It'll take me about an hour to drive there and another hour to drive back. Is there any way you can go to the showing instead?"

"No. I have that meeting with a client tonight. Remember? Can't you reschedule for another day?"

"Not until Friday. The property will probably be sold by then. Brett said it was one of the few homes left in the area. I checked it out online. It looks promising. I don't want to lose this chance, Megan. It might be the one."

Just what I needed—a blip in my schedule. "What time is the showing again?"

"Seven o'clock. You don't have to stay there long. Half an hour tops."

"I'll try to postpone my meeting. I'll call my client and see if I can reschedule."

"Thanks, Megan. Send me a text message if it's a go. I'll send you the address, then I'll call Brett to let him know you'll be meeting with him instead."

"Okay."

I called my client. She agreed to meet with me at eight o'clock. I sent Michael a text message to confirm I'd attend the house showing tonight and call him afterward to let him know how it went.

I'd just returned home after a lengthy drive in traffic when my phone rang. The display read: MTL-RES Group. The real estate company. I answered.

Ken Reilly introduced himself as a real estate agent with the firm. "I'm calling to let you know about a property for viewing tonight."

Here I was, rushing around to accommodate everyone, delaying my own work, and these agents couldn't even coordinate their schedules. I swallowed my annoyance and said, "I'm already meeting with an agent from your firm for a house showing tonight."

"That's right," Ken said. "But I'm calling about another house. A two-story home on Parkhurst Street recently came up. We're only contacting select buyers. The property isn't listed on the MLS."

Not on the Multiple Listing Service? It meant fewer buyers knew about it, which gave Michael and me an advantage.

Even so, Ken's intervention bothered me. Although it was obvious that he was calling me from MRG, I erred on the side of caution and asked, "How did you get my phone number?"

"I called Michael first," he said.

My guard was up. I doubted Michael would have given out my phone number without telling me about it. "Really?"

Ken continued. "I heard he was looking for a house in the area."

"Where did you hear that?"

"From my colleague, Brett Paquette."

While real estate agents were known to share leads about potential buyers and sellers, it struck me as odd that Brett would share us with another agent without letting Michael or me know beforehand. Maybe the hot real estate market was a factor. Then again, if it got us the house we wanted...

Ken went on. "When I told Michael about the showing, he sounded interested but said he couldn't make it. He asked me to call you."

That much was true. "What time is the showing?"

"Six o'clock."

I checked the time. Five-thirty. It was going to be tight. "Okay, I can make it. What's the address?"

"It's 246 Parkhurst Street. I'll meet you there. Bye."

I immediately entered the details on my phone and in my agenda next to six o'clock. My double foolproof system for keeping records. With two back-to-back showings and a client meeting, it promised to be a hectic evening. I didn't have time for dinner—not that there was much to choose from in the fridge—but I could grab a sandwich between showings.

An uneasy feeling swept over me. I felt uncomfortable about going to view a house with an agent I didn't know. I was about to call Michael to verify Ken's call but realized when reaching for my phone that he was on his way to meet with his informant. Besides, if Ken had my phone number, Michael had obviously given it to him.

Stop being so paranoid, I chided myself. I could simply add an extra layer of security by verifying Ken's validity online—something I could do without bothering Michael.

My phone rang, and I glanced at the screen. It was my mother. Oh, no! I'd forgotten to call her back about her dinner invitation tomorrow night.

I was running late. My mother loved to chat, so I didn't answer and let it go to voice mail. I'd call her back tonight when we'd have more time to catch up. I needed to talk to Michael about her dinner invitation anyway—something I'd neglected to do.

With a minute to spare, I googled the MTL-RES Group website. Ken Reilly's photo and bio confirmed he'd been working at the real estate agency for several years. As he mentioned, the home I was scheduled to visit tonight wasn't listed on the MLS with the other properties for sale.

Okay. I'd done my homework. Better safe than sorry.

3

MEGAN

Tuesday evening

The two-story gray stone townhouse on Parkhurst Street stood loftily among other 19th-Century homes. It was an impressive structure, but it didn't have a garage. One garage, but preferably two, was a feature Michael and I had specified in our requests to MRG. Maybe Michael thought the home had other benefits that were too good to pass up.

On the other hand, I was surprised he'd agreed to view a house that appeared to be even older than the one we'd visited earlier today. I'd forgotten to ask Ken if renovations or updates had been made to the property over the years. I made a mental note to ask him later.

I parked on the street and looked out the passenger window. A young woman was leading a little girl up the stairs to the front door of the house. It was unusual that the owner would be home while a prospective buyer dropped in for a showing. Another niggling detail.

I stepped out of the car.

"Megan!" a male voice called out.

I turned to see a dark-haired man in a black jacket and beige khakis get out of a car parked behind mine. He held a bouquet of flowers and waved at me.

As he approached, his amber sunglasses reflected the late September sun. "Hi, Megan. I'm Ken. These flowers are for you. A token of my appreciation." He smiled and handed me the bouquet.

"Oh...thanks." Did he offer flowers to every potential client he met?

"My pleasure. I hope it makes up for having you rush over here at the last minute."

I decided grace was the best approach. "It was hard to refuse the showing. The fact it isn't on the MLS is a plus." I pointed toward the house where I'd seen the woman and child. "Is the owner home?"

He grinned apologetically. "Actually, this is the wrong house. When I got here, I realized I'd made a mistake with the street name. The house we're visiting is on Parkvale Street. It's a couple of blocks over." He gestured in that direction, the keys on his MRG keychain jiggling in the air.

Despite his apparent validity, my guard was up again. My pulse quickened. Did he expect me to get in his car? I stalled. "How old is the house on Parkvale Street?"

"Not as old as this one," Ken said with a chuckle. "I know you and Michael want something more recent. I'll lead the way there. You can follow me in your car."

His answer reassured me. I exhaled, not realizing I'd been holding my breath.

~

The two-story red brick home with two garages looked inviting yet expensive. The lot was sprawling, with more than fifty feet between neighboring properties on each side. Houses in this area were valued in the million-dollar range.

Would Michael and I have to sell our souls to afford this house?

Ken led the way up a short flight of stairs. "Seems like there's some interest already." He motioned toward the driveway where two cars were parked.

"I thought this was a private showing," I said.

"It is," he said over his shoulder. "It's an impromptu open house for a select list of buyers."

Competition. An encouraging sign.

Ken removed his sunglasses and opened the front door. It squeaked. "A drop of oil will fix that." He chuckled.

For no reason other than curiosity, I asked, "Is the owner home?"

"No." He closed the door behind us. "The owner passed away. A relative arranged to hold the showing."

We crossed an expansive ceramic-tiled foyer lit by a crystal chandelier in the high-ceilinged space. An elegant touch. A peek into the den on the left revealed wall-to wall shelves of books, some of which were as dated as the vintage furniture occupying the room. I would have loved to browse through the books and wondered if the seller might accept to part with a few of them.

An antique writing desk sat in a niche beside an elaborate wood staircase that curved upwards. It was a beautiful piece and added interest to the foyer. Michael would love it.

Soft voices reached us even before we veered to the right into the living room. A short blonde woman in heels smiled at us, then moved through an archway and turned left down a corridor. An older man holding a glass of wine followed her out.

The home showing was so exclusive. I'd never experienced a showing where alcohol was served. I felt out of my league. And my comfort zone.

"Wine?" Ken asked me. He indicated a cocktail table where

two bottles of white wine chilled in stainless steel ice buckets and empty glasses waited to be filled.

"No, thanks," I said. "I have to drive somewhere else after."

"Same here."

I scanned the room. It boasted varnished wood floors and a high ceiling. Provincial-style sofas graced the space.

"You'll find wood floors and high ceilings throughout the house," Ken said. "The rooms are fully furnished, mostly with old-style décor as you can see."

"Is the furniture included in the selling price of the house?"

"I don't know. Would you like me to find out?"

"Sure." I was already visualizing how much fun Michael and I would have trying to blend the old with the new.

As Ken led me toward the archway, his phone rang. He dug it out of his pocket. "Excuse me. I have to take this call." He walked back into the foyer.

The creaking of floors upstairs meant more people were visiting. Judging from the empty glasses on a corner table, a handful of visitors had already come and gone.

I was eager to see the rest of the house, but Ken was still on the phone. It would be rude to move on without him, so I opted to hang around a bit longer.

An older couple entered the room through the archway and abandoned their wine glasses before heading out. That another agent wasn't accompanying them meant nothing. They could end up making an offer on the house anyway.

A pang of disappointment shot through me. What if a bidding war developed? Though I doubted Michael and I could afford the house, my interest in this place was mounting by the second.

Ken strolled up to me. "I have to go get some papers in the car. Feel free to look around, Megan."

"Okay." I moved through the archway, then thought about asking Ken if any renovations had been made to the house.

I retraced my steps and stopped when I saw him open a

drawer in the writing desk. He grabbed a white envelope and slid it in his jacket pocket, then rushed out the front door.

I didn't know what to make of his sneaky exit. Maybe the relative handling the sale had left him instructions or information about the house. If so, why hadn't he opened the envelope to see what was inside?

I let it go. It wasn't my business anyway.

I strolled back through the living room, then drifted under the archway and into the corridor. I passed a sitting room with a sofa and widescreen TV, another den, and another sitting room with more bookshelves. Another archway and connecting corridor eventually took me to the kitchen at the back of the house. The veritable maze of rooms astounded me. I'd need a road map to find my way back to the foyer!

The kitchen had been updated to include modern white cupboards and stainless-steel appliances and fixtures. A large island stood in the center of the room. Cozy bench seating in a corner by a window offered a view of tall red maple trees.

I imagined having coffee with Michael every morning in this charming kitchen. Yes, I could get used to that. The renovated kitchen was a definite plus in my book.

A glass-paned door at the far end opened up onto a sunroom. Windows looked out onto the backyard where a row of tall cedars formed a natural barrier between the property and neighboring lots. A spacious pond with a stone waterfall and a wooden pergola over a patio provided the perfect setting for outdoor entertaining.

I hadn't seen the rest of the house, but I was already sold on it and decided Michael had to see it. I was worried that the selling price might be completely out of our affordability range, but Michael did say he'd make an exception and use part of his inheritance money for a down payment. With a bit of luck, we might be able to negotiate a fair price.

I couldn't wait any longer. I had to share my excitement with him right now. I retrieved my phone from my handbag. If he didn't answer, I'd leave a message.

My phone indicated the battery was almost dead. In my haste to leave the condo, I'd forgotten to charge my phone.

The floor creaked behind me.

I glanced over my shoulder expecting to see Ken. Instead I saw a hairy man the size of a gorilla rushing toward me. He wore a gas mask and aimed a gadget at me.

I stepped back and screamed.

A puff of something hit my face.

I blacked out.

4

MICHAEL

Tuesday evening

Michael glanced at his watch. Seven o'clock.

Raoul Levesque, his informant, was an hour late.

He'd set up the meeting with Raoul by phone this afternoon. Although he hadn't met the guy before, he was impressed by his familiarity with the criminal operations of the Hells Angels. Raoul promised Michael he'd share inside information about the gang's latest plans and the names of key players involved.

Michael welcomed any facts that could contribute to the investigative article he was working on for *The Gazette*. The piece included the drug-trafficking activities of the Hells Angels and their attempts to fix the price of illegal drugs sold to the markets in Canada and abroad. He hadn't had a decent lead in weeks. Maybe Raoul would provide it.

He surveyed the people in the West End Pub. Located in a suburban neighborhood in the western end of the island of Montreal, the pub was crowded with patrons watching the Sports Network on overhead TVs. Busy and noisy. The perfect setting for a meeting with an informant. No one would pay attention to a discussion between two unfamiliar men sitting in a shadowy corner.

Michael had arrived at six to find the place already packed. He'd been lucky to get a table at the back of the floor. He'd waited half an hour, but when Raoul still hadn't shown up, he ordered dinner. He was hungry and didn't owe anyone an excuse for eating.

His mind drifted back to the Hells Angels. His journalistic mission had long focused on breaking up their illegal drug-trafficking operations. He'd had a relative degree of success owing to informants who had supplied him with critical data about the gang over the years, but several of them had let him down. Either they hadn't shown up, or the facts they'd provided had turned out to be erroneous. He didn't want to raise his hopes about Raoul. Yet he kept glancing at the entrance, expecting him to show up at any moment.

He checked the time. Seven-thirty.

He picked up his phone. The racket in this place could have caused him to miss his call or text message.

No. Nothing from him.

He called Raoul's number, but the guy didn't pick up. Maybe he was driving and didn't have a hands-free option in his car. He left Raoul a message saying he'd be leaving the pub at eight o'clock.

No messages from Megan either. He'd received her text message this afternoon confirming she was going to the house showing at seven o'clock. He was grateful she'd postponed her client meeting till eight. He owed her a big one.

He checked the time again. Megan should have visited the house on Hillside Avenue by now. She said she'd call as soon as she left the showing, which he calculated was between seven-thirty and eight o'clock.

On impulse, he called her. She didn't answer. Maybe she was already in a meeting with her client and didn't want to be disturbed. She'd probably turned her phone off. He left a message anyway.

Back to Raoul. Another fifteen minutes had passed. By now Michael was convinced he was a no-show. Either something unfortunate had happened to the guy, or Michael had been taken for a ride. He'd hate to think it was either.

Frustrated, he hurriedly paid the tab for his dinner and left.

Traffic was light on the drive back to Montreal. Michael swung into an all-night store in Westmount and picked up a carton of milk and a dozen eggs. He was inspecting the expiry date on a package of Havarti cheese when he felt someone's eyes on him.

A petite blonde woman gave him a wide smile, then hastily turned away. As she pushed her cart laden with groceries down the aisle, he watched her.

Now *he* was doing the staring. What the hell was wrong with him? A strange woman had found him attractive. So what?

He paid for his groceries and returned to the car. A cold gust of wind tickled his neck, and he raised the collar of his jacket. In two months, the white stuff would be falling from the sky.

He got behind the steering wheel and checked his phone for the umpteenth time tonight. No messages. Strange. It was almost nine o'clock. He should have heard from Megan by now.

Where was she?

~

The condo was dark.

Megan was adamant about having at least two lights on at night: the corner lamp in the living room and the night light in the hallway.

Michael turned the light on in the entrance. "Megan," he called out.

No answer.

Maybe she was asleep.

He tiptoed to the bedroom and flipped the light switch. The bed was neatly made up.

He went through the same routine for each room before he moved on to the kitchen. He deposited the bag of groceries on the counter, then placed the milk, eggs, and cheese in the fridge.

Megan.

Her eight o'clock meeting with her client could have lasted longer than she'd anticipated. She had to deal with difficult clients at times. He'd hear all about it when she'd come home from a meeting, exhausted after having explained at length to the client that no, she couldn't write his or her memoir in a week, or yes, you might get sued if you intentionally write something malicious about a real person in your book.

Michael pulled out his phone and called Bradford Publishing. Megan had access to a conference room there where she occasionally met with clients to discuss projects the firm assigned to her. It was possible she'd met with her client there. Another possibility: Other co-workers could have been involved in the project, and they all stayed behind afterward to chat.

But no one picked up at Bradford, and his call went to voice mail. He left a message.

Michael pondered another scenario. Megan might have visited her mother in town. He scanned his contact list for Mrs. Sullivan's number—or Connie, as she preferred to be called.

"No, Megan's not here," Connie said, concern in her voice. "I'm waiting to hear from her about dinner tomorrow night. She was supposed to call me back to let me know if you both could make it."

Michael didn't know anything about the dinner. Swamped with her job and house-hunting outings, Megan had evidently forgotten to mention it to him.

He didn't want to cause Connie unnecessary stress. Megan had confided that her mother had developed high blood pressure and needed to take things easy. That their condo was a brief drive away allayed Megan's worries about her mother's health. It was one of the reasons they wanted to buy a home nearby.

"She was meeting with a client tonight," Michael said. "She might still be at Bradford Publishing. I called there and left a message."

"Thank you, Michael," she said. "You know how much I worry about her."

With good reason. He'd shared her anguish after Megan's husband had been murdered. The nightmare had intensified when his cold-blooded killer had pursued Megan and tried to murder her.

"I'll let you know as soon as I hear from her," Michael said before he ended the call.

He sat on the couch in the living room and caught the ten o'clock news on TV. He tried to concentrate, but his mind kept wandering off. He flipped aimlessly from station to station, not finding anything that interested him.

He tried to reason with himself, convince himself that although Megan's meeting had dragged on for more than an hour, a two-hour meeting with a client wasn't out of the ordinary. He'd often spent hours discussing upcoming articles with his editor at *The Gazette.* He would wait a while longer. Megan might walk in at any moment or reply to one of the messages he'd sent her.

He brewed a pot of coffee, then opened his laptop on the kitchen table. He'd been doing the legwork on the Hells Angels article for months now. The infamous gang had set up networks for trafficking illegal drugs—like fentanyl—across the country. Through his investigative articles, Michael was doing his part to inform the public about the rising fentanyl crisis. And he felt pretty good about it.

Not all the information he'd gathered was based on research. He'd garnered part of it from personal observation.

Like the time he'd witnessed a young guy collapse on the street after he'd unwittingly taken fentanyl. He was certain the guy had no pulse, but paramedics brought him back to life with a shot of naloxone. Statistics showed that thousands of others hadn't been as lucky. Michael hoped his articles would increase public awareness about the escalating drug problem and save lives.

His thoughts flashed back to Raoul as he sipped his coffee. He was frustrated that the informant hadn't shown up at the pub. He'd pinned his expectations on him to provide updates on the Hells Angels' illegal drug activities. As Michael had often done, he'd planned to pass along any pertinent details to the cops to assist in closing down those operations.

Maybe Raoul got cold feet at the last minute. It happened. Talking to reporters or cops was risky, and leaks to the wrong people could expose an informant as a rat. The consequences were sometimes fatal.

Michael tried to concentrate on his article, but no matter what he wrote, he deleted it seconds later. Something else was bothering him.

Megan.

Before the clock struck eleven, his worry meter soared. He ignored it. He hadn't run out of options yet.

He poured more coffee into his cup, then phoned Brett Paquette, his real estate agent. Brett was usually on call—even after regular business hours.

"Hey, Michael." Brett's cheery voice came through. "What can I do for you?"

"I'm following up on the house showing you arranged for Megan at seven tonight. A two-story on Hillside Avenue."

"Oh, yeah. Too bad she couldn't make it."

Michael spilled some coffee on the kitchen table. "What? She told me she was going." He reached for a paper towel and wiped up the spill.

"She sent me a text message about half an hour before the

scheduled time and canceled," Brett said. "I figured she changed her mind."

"Did she give you a reason?"

"No. She said you'd reschedule with me later. Did you want to do that now?"

Michael's trepidation spiked. "Could another agent have approached her for the showing instead?"

"I didn't ask anyone to go in my place." Brett paused. "You sound edgy. What's up?"

If he'd been dealing with anyone else, Michael would have told him to mind his own business. But the men had known each other for years, starting with the day Michael first contacted Brett to find the condominium he now shared with Megan. Since then, they occasionally met up for early morning runs in the neighborhood.

"Megan hasn't come home," Michael said. "The last time I heard from her was when she sent me a text message to confirm she was going to your house showing. She had an eight o'clock meeting with a client afterward." He glanced at his watch. "It's eleven o'clock. It's not like her to stay out of touch this long. I've called everyone I know, and they haven't heard from her either."

"Maybe she went out for coffee with friends," Brett offered.

Michael didn't think so, but he didn't feel like explaining his reasoning behind it. "Yeah. I'll give it more time. Thanks, Brett."

He appreciated Brett's encouragement, but no one knew Megan's habits better than he did. She would have alerted him about any change in her plans. Had the situation been reversed, he would have done the same. They had an unspoken pact, one they initiated after her husband was murdered.

He contemplated his next move. He regretted he hadn't taken the time to go to the home showing. Now Megan was missing. And all because of that informant who didn't show up. Damn him!

He told Megan the email he'd received this morning before he left the condo was a meeting reminder. He'd lied.

It was the same anonymous message he'd received once before: *Vengeance.* A simple word that was threatening and hostile, yet allusive. He didn't want to link the ominous message to Megan's disappearance, but the timing was too close to be a coincidence.

His instincts kicked in in full force.

Megan hadn't returned his calls.

Something was seriously wrong.

5

———

MEGAN

Tuesday night

Darkness flooded the space around me. There was no noise.

I was lying on my back and felt lightheaded. My mouth was dry. My hands were taped in front of me so tightly that I feared my blood would stop circulating.

The surface beneath me—a thin carpet—provided a flimsy barrier to the cold, hard floor. The air smelled of dampness and something else. Paint?

I shifted my position and tried to move my feet, but something weighted them down. I tried again. A metal chain clanked against what sounded like a cement floor. I sat up and stretched my bound hands down to my legs. Chains were fastened around my ankles!

I swung my legs to one side and met resistance. The chains were anchored to something. The floor? A wall?

My head was pounding—no doubt from the substance the gorilla man had sprayed in my face. I must have passed out because I had no recollection of what happened afterward.

How long ago was that? And where was I?

I had driven to a home showing. A real estate agent met me there. Ken Reilly. Yes, that was his name. Where was he?

I listened. It was eerily quiet.

I slowly twisted my body around and stared into the dark. I noticed two narrow slits of light. One was on my right, higher up. The other was ahead of me but much further away. Windows? Was I in a basement?

It would explain the cement floor, the windows above ground level. There were definitely cans of paint down here. Was I in the same house I'd visited for the home showing?

One thing was indisputable: I was in a cold, murky place and was being held here against my will.

The image of the gorilla man whizzed through my mind, and I trembled. Massive and hairy, the alias suited him well. That big hulk was strong enough to have carried me downstairs after he'd sprayed me with heaven-knew-what that knocked me out.

Who was he and why had he kidnapped me?

Ken told me the owner of the house had passed away. Was the gorilla man the relative handling the sale of the house?

Or was he a wayward stranger who'd walked in off the street in search of a victim? Ken or anyone else would certainly have noticed if he'd carried me out of the house.

Maybe I was still in the same house I'd visited on Parkvale Street. The spacious old house with the stacks of books and maze of archways and lovely white kitchen and tall cedar shrubs...

What if the gorilla man had been hired to abduct me? He could have waited until everyone else had left the house, then used a chemical gas to knock me out and keep me prisoner here.

But why would he want to kidnap me? Why would anyone want to kidnap me? I wasn't wealthy enough for a lucrative ransom payoff.

Michael.

Maybe it had something to do with him. As a journalist, he'd rubbed certain people the wrong way—especially felons. Was the gorilla man someone he'd helped put in jail?

I turned my head too quickly and felt woozy. Probably the residual effect of the gas.

I took a deep breath. The dizziness subsided a bit, but my thoughts were foggy. I had to think back...way back...

Ken Reilly. He'd met me at the address on Parkhurst Street. He claimed he'd made a mistake and then redirected me to the house on Parkvale Street. Other potential buyers were attending the showing, drinking wine, walking about...

It seemed unusual that something would have happened to me there, but I had no other explanation. I definitely didn't make it to the second house showing to meet Brett Paquette...

Wait a sec. Why hadn't Ken returned after he went to fetch the papers in his car? If he had, he would have noticed I'd disappeared. Wouldn't he have wondered where I was if my car was still parked in front of the house?

Had the gorilla man knocked him out and kidnapped him too? Was Ken down here with me?

There was only one way to find out. "Ken, are you here? Ken?"

No response.

The last I saw of Ken was when he removed an envelope from the desk in the foyer. What was in it? Was it a payoff? Is that why he didn't return?

Had Ken played a part in my kidnapping?

All those suspicions I'd had about him from the start...

My blunder hit me with the force of a sledgehammer.

Oh, my God! I'd walked right into a trap!

I felt sick to my stomach and swallowed hard.

What if my abductors had gone and left me here, with no intent to return? In the basement of an unoccupied house, I could die, and no one would ever find me.

My heart beat faster. "Help!" I yelled. "Somebody, help me!" I screamed as loud as I could.

Nothing. Just silence.

I swallowed hard.

Michael.

An image of him popped into my mind, how those blue eyes smiled at me and understood my every thought... The hunky way all six feet of him filled his T-shirt and cargoes... All the things we planned to do together, all our unfulfilled dreams...

Michael must have figured out by now that something awful happened to me. How on earth would he ever find me? Despairing that I'd never see him again, I burst into tears.

I cried for a minute or two. Okay, enough self-pity. I had to stop feeling sorry for myself. It wasn't in my nature to give up so easily. I was a fighter. I raised my bound hands and wiped the tears from my cheeks.

Logic. I had to draw on logic. Maybe there was a grander motive behind my abduction, and I was basically the means to an end.

Was it part of a ransom plot to obtain money from Michael? Few people knew that he came from a wealthy family, but even criminals did background checks. Was the culprit an enemy—one of the numerous lawbreakers he'd investigated and helped prosecute in court? Or was it someone he'd once considered a friend, now turned jealous rival?

Whoever had planned this venture had to have known Michael and me personally or done their research on us. I kept returning to the likelihood it was someone he'd helped put in jail, someone who was looking for revenge. If so, the list of suspects was long—and dangerous. Had one of them followed me around? Tracked my daily routine?

I'd spent a lot of time in sessions with a therapist after my husband was killed and his murderer began to stalk me. I'd taken extra precautions since then to ensure that no one was following me or had a chance to lure me into a compromising situation.

Where had I screwed up?

I'd established Ken Reilly's validity at MRG, but I hadn't called Michael to verify the showing with him. Then again, why wouldn't I trust Ken? He was a real estate agent. The MRG website confirmed that he worked there. Their agents were supposed to be reputable people who adhered to a code of ethics.

Granted, there was no For Sale sign on the front lawn of the Parkvale Street home, but Ken had said it was a recent addition to the market and only select buyers had been contacted for the showing.

Ken said the house was on Parkhurst Street when he'd initially called me. Damn. That was the house I'd looked up online—not the house on Parkvale Street.

It didn't matter. Ken told me the Parkvale home wasn't listed on the MLS anyway. The street names were similar, so he could have made a simple mistake. In the end, other people had arrived to view the house, so it had to be a legitimate showing. Right?

So where did I go so wrong?

I'd confirmed Ken's association with MRG and made a rational decision to meet with him. Besides, it wasn't as if I had to get Michael's approval for every decision I made. If I had to live that way, I wouldn't accomplish anything.

Yet, here I was.

And it was all my fault. A bad decision had led me here, and I had to find a way to get out of this horrific situation.

But I wasn't alone. Michael would come looking for me once Brett Paquette told him I was a no-show. He would find me and rescue me. I had to believe it with all my heart, or else I'd go nuts.

Something skimmed across my hands. Something light and leggy. I shuddered.

Spiders weren't on my list of favorite things. This place might be filled with them—and other creepy crawlies.

A single bulb lit up the ceiling.

My initial suspicions were correct. I was in a basement.

A door creaked open at the top of the stairs.

Voices reached me. A man and a woman.

I didn't recognize either one.

6

———

MICHAEL

Tuesday night

Michael revised his plan to report Megan's disappearance to the police officer on night duty. Convinced that foul play was involved, he abandoned the idea of a phone call and drove to the police station to speak with Detective Sergeant Pete Esposito instead.

He'd enjoyed his ride-along experiences last summer with Esposito and the Montreal Police. He'd witnessed how the middle-aged detective preferred to use his wits rather than weapons to persuade criminals to surrender. He respected that.

Like the time the SWAT team detained an adult and two nervous juveniles who were manufacturing illegal drugs in the basement of a suburban house. Esposito had persuaded one of the boys to put down the knife he was brandishing. By doing so, he'd probably prevented the kid from embarking on a life of crime and ensuing jail terms.

Michael parked the car on the street, then strode into the police station and asked to see Esposito. His instincts had served him well. The detective was on duty.

Esposito invited him to take a seat across from his desk in the open-concept office. He gestured toward the coffee machine on a counter along the wall. "Would you like a cup?"

Michael's stomach churned from the three cups of coffee he'd gulped down while waiting for Megan to arrive. Or was it a case of jittery nerves? If anything, he needed to remain calm. "No, thanks."

The detective sat down and leaned back in his chair. "The last time we met, you shared drug-trafficking info on the Hells Angels that proved extremely useful. You have something new for us?"

"Unfortunately, no. I set up a meeting with an informant earlier, but he didn't show up. I'm here on a personal matter tonight."

"Oh." Esposito raised an eyebrow. "What can I do for you?"

Michael recounted the events of the evening and his qualms about Megan's disappearance.

Esposito reached for a pen and notepad. "For the record, where were you earlier tonight?"

Michael detailed the timeline involving his trip to the pub and back. "By the time I got home, I still hadn't heard from Megan."

"You think something unfortunate might have happened to her?"

"My gut tells me yes." He leaned forward. "It's not like Megan to be out at this time of the night without letting me know where she is. It's not like her to avoid answering my phone calls or replying to my text messages either."

Esposito's dark eyes studied him. "You're not one of those possessive boyfriends who insist on keeping tabs on their girl-friends, are you?"

"Not at all. Megan is open about sharing her whereabouts with me. She feels safer when she does." He paused. "I told you about Megan's history before—about her husband's murder and the killer who tailed her afterward."

Esposito nodded. "I was stationed elsewhere when it hit the papers, but I remember reading about that Montreal case years ago."

"Believe me, it's as fresh in my mind as if it happened yesterday," Michael said. "That traumatic event is the reason behind Megan's insecurity."

"Before we take any action, we need to eliminate other potential reasons behind her disappearance. Does she have a medical condition that you know of? Any lapse of memory experiences, for example?"

"No and no. She has a terrific memory."

"Any relatives she might be visiting?"

"She has no relatives here, except for her mother who lives in town. I talked to her this evening. She said she was expecting a call from Megan but hadn't heard from her. She lives alone, so Megan keeps in touch with her every day."

"I see." Esposito joined his hands to form a steeple. "How about enemies?"

"Megan has no enemies."

"But you do."

"What crime reporter doesn't? I could give you a list the length of my arm."

"Do it," Esposito said. "Prepare a list of your top potential suspects for me. Names, crimes committed... I'll run a check on them." He briefly glanced away. "Here's what we're going to do. Although we're only talking hours since you claim Megan went missing, I can see where a break in her routine would raise a red flag."

"You got that right," Michael said.

"Based on the unusual circumstances, we'll file a missing person report ASAP." Esposito pulled out a blank report from a drawer in his desk. "Would you have a recent photo of Megan? A description of her car?"

Michael showed him the photos he'd stored on his phone.

"Send them to me by email."

He already had Esposito's email address on file. "Done. Megan has a GPS tracker on her car."

"Good. What was she wearing when you last saw her?"

"I don't know. Maybe a jacket and pants. She might have changed before her other meetings later in the day. She does that sometimes."

"I'll need her cell phone number, email address... Any other links."

Michael gave him the details.

"You know the drill," the detective said. "Backtrack and give me the events of the day as they relate to your interactions with Megan."

Michael began with the home showing that he and Megan had attended in the morning. He described Megan's text message confirming she was going to meet Brett Paquette at seven in the evening for a house showing on Hillside Avenue. He finished off with her client meeting at eight—possibly held at Bradford Publishing.

"Does Megan have a contact that you know of at Bradford?" Esposito asked.

"Kayla Warren. She's the project manager there." Michael read out the company's phone number and address.

The detective jotted the information. "What about the house showing that Megan was supposed to go to tonight?"

"When I called Brett at MRG earlier, he told me she'd canceled with him and didn't reschedule. Megan didn't tell me."

Esposito scribbled more notes. "So it's out of the ordinary. That she didn't tell you about her change in plans, I mean."

Michael maintained a composed demeanor, even though the tension inside him hadn't subsided since his arrival at the station. "Like I said, it's highly unusual."

The detective sat back in his chair. "Did you and Megan have an argument recently?"

"No."

"A misunderstanding about something?"

Michael shrugged. "She wasn't enthusiastic about visiting the house tonight because she couldn't fit it into her schedule at first. She sent me a text message later to confirm she'd pushed back a client meeting to eight o'clock so she could go to the showing."

"Do you have that message?"

"Yes." Michael retrieved it on his phone to show him.

"Did you keep any other messages she sent you?"

"I usually delete them, but I might have a couple."

"Send me everything you have."

Michael was beginning to feel like a suspect, but he understood that Esposito's request was based on protocol. He was also aware that the police could gain access to his phone at any time if their request was warranted. He immediately forwarded Megan's emails and text messages to the detective.

"There's something else," Michael said. "Whoever is behind Megan's disappearance might be the same person sending me threatening messages. Vengeance is the word of the day." He accessed the emails on his phone and showed them to Esposito. "I don't speak much French, but I know the word is spelled the same way in English or French. Language has no barriers when it comes to retaliation from the criminals I helped put in jail."

Esposito looked them over. "We can do a trace—"

"Don't bother. They were sent from disposable phones or short-lived email addresses. Happens all the time."

"And you know this how?"

"I have my sources. And I protect them."

"I know you do." Esposito tapped the report. "We'll get this information on Megan out to the field ASAP. In the meantime, go over her things at home to see if anything is missing."

Michael stared at him. "Missing?"

"Clothes...personal items. Maybe there was another reason she initially hesitated about going to the house showing." Esposito threw him a probing look.

"You think she left me?"

"Some people don't know how to end things. They just walk away."

"Not Megan. She wouldn't do that to me." Michael's jaw tightened. Esposito didn't know Megan the way he did. "We're wasting time. Megan could be out there somewhere, alone, injured."

No reaction from Esposito meant he wasn't convinced. "Consider my theory anyway. It happens more often than you can imagine." He softened his approach. "Look, there could be a valid reason for Megan's disappearance. Maybe something was bothering her, and she's talking it over with a close friend. From my experience as a married man, women don't always say what's on their minds."

That Megan might be unhappy in their relationship had never occurred to Michael. She verbalized her feelings and didn't hold back from expressing them—especially when she disagreed with him. Only this morning, she'd lambasted him for taking on riskier assignments. She claimed he was trying to prove his worth to his parents and suggested they go visit them. He admired her attempt to patch things up between his father and him, but it wasn't going to happen.

"It's not like that between Megan and me," Michael said. "We're open with each other." He realized he sounded defensive. "Sorry. I can't help worrying—"

"It's early yet. She might still show up tonight." Esposito rose to his feet. "If you hear from her—no matter what time it is —please call me."

Michael stood up. "No problem. What's your next move?" Normally he wouldn't have dared to be so direct, but he figured Esposito owed him for the times he passed along reliable street information to him.

"I'll call Brett Paquette at MRG. I'll visit the Hillside Avenue address Megan had booked with him for the seven o'clock showing and speak with the owners. Maybe she had a change of heart and went to visit the house on her own."

"I'd like to go with you."

Esposito raised a forefinger. "Let's get one thing straight. This case hits too close to home for you to get involved. Stay out of it, Michael."

Back at the condo, Michael combed through the closet in the main bedroom. From what he could tell, there was nothing missing in Megan's wardrobe to indicate she'd packed a suitcase. There were several empty hangers, but that was normal. Washday was on the weekend, and the laundry basket already contained items.

Esposito had asked him what Megan might have been wearing when she left the house later today. As he skimmed through the clothes in her wardrobe, it was evident that he wouldn't be able to tell him if his life depended on it. Did other guys pay attention to this kind of stuff? It didn't matter. Guilt swept over him anyway.

He searched Megan's dresser drawers next. Nothing seemed to be missing. He reasoned that, if she'd left him, she'd have packed a supply of underwear. What woman would leave behind expensive, lacy things like the ones he'd bought her at Christmas and on her birthday?

He moved to the ensuite bathroom and opened the cabinets and drawers. Although it wasn't his habit to keep track of Megan's toiletries, cosmetics, and perfumes, there were no empty spaces to indicate she'd removed a bunch of items.

He made his way along the corridor to Megan's office. He'd grown accustomed to seeing sticky notes on her desk and around her computer screen. They were indications of her work in progress. He could tell when her schedule was hectic by the increasing number of yellow, pink, and blue sticky notes decorating her workspace—signs of the various projects she was working on.

He examined the larger notes on her desk. They contained facts about file edits and other publishing details. The smaller notes on her computer screen specified urgent and less urgent timelines. Nothing out of the ordinary.

He peered at her open agenda and scanned the day's notes. Above the seven o'clock appointment with Brett was another entry. It read: Six o'clock—house showing at 246 Parkhurst Street.

What the hell?

7

———

MEGAN

Tuesday night

The solitary light bulb in the basement ceiling shed a faint glow over my surroundings. At the top of the stairs, a muted conversation ensued between a man and a woman whose voices were unfamiliar to me.

I swiftly glanced around. The narrow slits I'd seen earlier were two ground-level windows—one at the back of the house and the other on the side. Thick darkening curtains had prevented most of the light from entering.

At the far end, half-painted drywall lined a wall. Cans of paint and brushes were abandoned, as if work had come to an abrupt end. It explained the smell. Tarps and plastic sheets randomly covered pieces of furniture and other objects piled along the wall on my right, casting shadows across the floor.

Closer at hand, a pile of trays held dishes and scraps of food. Someone had been eating down here. Had they watched me while I'd lain unconscious on the tattered carpet?

I shuddered.

A short chain linking my ankle restraints was bolted to the

floor next to the cement wall a few feet from me. Dust along the base of the wall had trapped spiders and other insects. I recoiled and moved as far away as I could.

My handbag was gone. No surprise there. My kidnappers had probably destroyed my cell phone so no one could trace my location.

Footsteps sounded on the stairs.

Someone was coming!

The thump of heavy feet grew louder with each descending step.

A chill ran down my spine as the gorilla man materialized holding a tray with two plates of food, a bottle of water, and a can of beer. He put the tray down on the floor.

He leaned toward me, his breath hot and foul, and I cringed. His tattered jeans and a T-shirt looked and smelled as if they hadn't been washed in days. His dirty hair and the dark stubble on his face intensified his unkempt appearance.

My stomach grew queasy. How much longer would I have to share the same space with someone so vile?

He straightened up and took out a pocketknife.

"No!" I recoiled in terror.

"Stop moving." He firmly gripped my hands and sliced through the tape.

I exhaled with relief.

"I brought you water and bread," he said. "If you scream, I'll punch you out. Promise to be good?"

I nodded. My heart beat so loudly in my chest that I was certain he could hear it.

He picked up a plate and bottle of water and placed them on the carpet close to me. "Now eat. No funny stuff. Understand?" His beady eyes protruded beneath a narrow forehead.

"Yes." I scrutinized the bottle of water and the slice of white bread topped with a thin spread of jam. As hungry as I was, I debated whether or not I should take a bite. What if the food contained poison?

Logic prevailed. If they wanted me dead, they'd have done it by now.

"Eat," the gorilla man urged again.

I took a few sips of water, then bit into the bread.

He stood there, staring down at me with a dumb expression on his face, almost as if he were waiting for me to toss him a morsel.

Or waiting to make sure I had swallowed the poison.

Between bites, I asked, "Where's Ken?"

He grimaced. "Huh?"

Was he as daft as he looked? "The real estate agent. Ken Reilly. He brought me here."

Without a word, he turned away and plodded toward the wall on the right. From under a tarp, he took hold of two metal folding chairs, opened them up, and set them facing each other. He walked back to get the tray and placed it on one of the chairs. He pulled back another tarp to reveal a flat screen TV, then reached for the remote and clicked it on.

I waited for him to say something about Ken once he completed his routine, but he didn't. I repeated my question. "Where's Ken?"

"Quiet." He put a finger to his lips.

While he dribbled a can of beer down his T-shirt and chewed loudly on two thick sandwiches, he intently watched contestants competing on a TV game show. Every time a contestant slid and fell into a pool, he sniggered loudly. It was a wonder the neighbors didn't hear his garish horselaughs—not to mention the disgusting burps he emitted.

Or maybe they did. Maybe the gorilla man lived here, and the neighbors were already familiar with his crude habits. I had to find out.

"Is this your house?" I asked him.

He scowled at me, then looked back at the TV.

I persisted. "Why am I here? What do you want from me?"

No reaction this time.

"Who is the woman upstairs?"

He pushed back his chair and reached me in two strides, the smell of beer floating in the air between us. He removed a pair of handcuffs from the back pocket of his jeans, pulled my arms behind me, and secured the handcuffs. He reached for a roll of duct tape on a ledge and used his pocketknife to cut off a long piece. "You talk too much."

"No, please don't. I haven't finished my—"

He clamped the bandage hard against my mouth, roughly flattening the edges against my cheeks. He cut two more pieces and applied them in an X across my mouth and cheeks to keep the first piece in place. Satisfied, he stomped back to his seat in front of the TV.

I'd blown it. When would I get another chance to talk to him? Worse yet, my mouth had been clamped in the nastiest way. I hadn't finished my slice of bread and regretted it. I was already starting to feel faint from lack of food.

Tears welled in my eyes, but I blinked them away. I refused to show any sign of weakness in front of this monster. I had dealt with all sorts of difficult people, but I had no idea how to deal with his detached cruelty.

The gorilla man kept his attention on the TV for the most part while he finished his meal but peeked at me from time to time. Did that big oaf actually think I'd try to run away?

"Lardo! Get up here!" a woman's throaty voice boomed from upstairs.

The gorilla man jumped to his feet, knocking over the tray and its contents. "Dang it!" He turned off the TV and slogged upstairs.

The light in the basement went off.

Lardo. Talk about a name. I almost felt sorry for him.

And who was that woman? Judging from Lardo's dutiful and prompt behavior, she was someone to be reckoned with.

Feet shuffled upstairs across the foyer.

More yelling by the woman.

The front door slammed shut.

Silence.

A car engine started up outside, died, then started up again. The starter on my car didn't always engage the first time. Were they driving off in my car?

Had they abandoned me, left me here to die alone?

Would anyone ever find me?

Even Michael had no idea where I was.

No! No! This can't be happening to me!

I tugged at the chain until my ankles hurt. The clamp didn't slacken.

I inched sideways toward the cement wall. I reached for the chain with my shackled hands and pulled, but it didn't give. I tried again. Useless.

If only it weren't so dark in here, I'd try to find something to pry the chain off my feet. Or at least scream for help. Lardo had cuffed my hands behind me, so I had to improvise.

I slid up to the cement wall and rubbed my cheeks against it in an attempt to remove the tape. If I ended up with scratches and scars, so be it.

But my efforts failed. My cheeks burned from rubbing them against the rough surface. I tried to open my mouth, but the pieces of tape held fast.

A dog was barking. It sounded close by—like at the side of the house. It was scratching at the window on my right!

I screamed! I rattled the chains with my feet. Then I screamed again.

The tape over my mouth muffled my cries, but a dog's hearing range was wider than a human's. There was a chance he could hear me.

He did. I could tell because he wouldn't stop barking and pawing at the window.

I screamed again and again. I rattled the chains until the muscles in my legs ached and I had to stop.

A woman's frail voice reached me. I strained to hear what

she was saying. The dog suddenly stopped barking and pawing at the window.

And they were gone.

A sense of vulnerability overwhelmed me.

Michael, where are you? Please help me!

He'd raised the subject of marriage this morning, and I'd shot it down. It wasn't the first time. Once again, I'd led Michael to believe that I didn't want to marry him. He thought I didn't have confidence in a future with him, that the nature and unpredictable hours of his investigative work would put a wedge between us.

But that wasn't the reason I didn't want to get married again.

I trusted Michael explicitly. The only person I didn't trust was myself. I didn't think I could marry someone who might unexpectedly leave me widowed again. My motives were selfish, and fear clouded my perception. For years, it had been hard to rise above these limitations.

Until I figured out a way to do it.

The upside of our relationship was that Michael welcomed my growing interest in his work, as well as my input. He asked me to accompany him on investigative ventures that he deemed less threatening—though they often turned out to be more ominous than we'd anticipated. What he didn't know was that I accepted his invitations not only because my own job was so boring but also because it gave me a chance to hold him back from taking unnecessary risks. It eased my qualms somewhat about his safety.

My plan wouldn't obliterate all my fears. If I wanted to come to grips with them, I had to accept that Michael was streetwise and capable of taking care of himself.

Which was a lot more than I could say about myself right now.

I'd made a serious mistake. I should have told Michael I'd planned on going to this earlier house showing.

House showing? What a farce! It was a setup from the start. I should have seen it coming.

Then again, I hadn't always been this wary. I could pinpoint the day I began to feel insecure about my surroundings. It was right after my husband's murder and the stalker episode. I developed a distrust of strangers and couldn't shake off the feeling that someone was following me. After years of therapy, I had finally succeeded in getting my life back to normal.

Even so, I hadn't attended any of the house showings alone. Michael and I had gone together. Despite the courageous front I tried to portray, a residue of doubt about my safety lingered.

Why did I have to go and show Michael that I was so brave? How would I ever manage to get out of here?

Michael must have contacted the police and reported me missing by now. He must have requested a trace on my car too. I had no doubt he was turning the city upside down looking for me. It was something he'd do without hesitation.

Exhaustion overcame me all of a sudden. My arms ached from the discomfort of having my hands tied behind my back. I lay down on my side and closed my eyes.

I tried to think positive thoughts. I envisioned the police stopping my car on the road and arresting Lardo and his female accomplice. They would question the culprits and then they'd find me...

But what if the police didn't stop them? What if those maniacs escaped police surveillance and left town?

No. It didn't make sense. What would they have to gain by leaving me here?

On the flip side, what if Lardo and the woman were coming back? Would they use me to extort ransom money from Michael? Or did they have more diabolical plans in store for me?

I shivered.

Was this the last day of my life?

8

———

MICHAEL

Wednesday morning

Megan!

Michael woke up with a start. He'd watched the late-night news and dozed off on the living room sofa waiting for Megan to return. Though he'd tossed and turned all night, it hadn't felt right to sleep in their bedroom without her by his side. His aching neck was a nasty byproduct of his decision.

Rays of sun sifted through the slats in the window blinds. He checked the time. Eight o'clock. He'd fallen asleep in the early morning hours and awakened from a terrifying dream about Megan. He couldn't remember the details, only that the atmosphere was gloomy.

He was a light sleeper and would have heard her come in last night. Yielding to the unlikely chance that he hadn't, he rushed down the hallway to the bedroom.

Their bed hadn't been slept in. The stark reminder that Megan was still missing sent a spasm through his gut. He'd replayed their recent conversations in his mind and reviewed her text messages last night on the chance that he'd missed a tiny detail. But he hadn't.

Guilt seeped through him. He regretted that he hadn't met Brett for the house showing on Hillside Avenue last evening. He'd driven across town to meet with an informant instead and asked Megan to go to the house showing in his place. He should have known better than to send her off alone. If he hadn't pressured her, she wouldn't have gone missing. It was all his fault.

He clenched his fists in anger. Damn!

He'd grudgingly heeded Esposito's warning about keeping his nose out of the investigation. He brooded at home while the detective interviewed the homeowners on Hillside Avenue and dropped by the Parkhurst Street address. That last stop troubled him. Why hadn't Megan told him she was going to a six o'clock showing there?

Esposito had called him back late last night to confirm that the Hillside Avenue showing had been canceled—like Brett had told Michael earlier. It followed that no prospective buyers had visited the house that night.

The Parkhurst Street homeowners told Esposito they hadn't returned from work until early evening and hadn't seen Megan or any suspicious activity in the neighborhood. Their nanny, however, had been at home all day with their daughter.

Esposito had tried to reach the young nanny on her cell phone, but she hadn't picked up. He'd visited her roommate who said the woman was out for the night with friends—she didn't know who—and didn't expect her back until morning.

The detective told Michael he planned to return to the house on Parkhurst Street first thing this morning to interview the nanny. He promised he'd keep in touch.

Michael rubbed his temples. He felt a headache coming on. He hadn't considered how vulnerable a target Megan might be in the eyes of enemies he'd made over the years. Megan had no enemies, but he did. Lots of them.

Who else could have enticed her away but a vindictive criminal who had it in for him, someone he'd helped put in jail? Even from behind bars, prisoners exerted power over individuals on the outside who did their bidding.

A handful of recent offenders came to mind—inmates who had the potential to harm him or anyone close to him through their elusive contacts. He'd lost a couple of reliable informants that way. No amount of time would erase the remorse he felt every time he remembered those who'd risked their lives for him. He'd used them to advance his interests, and even though they'd willingly shared information with him about those on the wrong side of the law, guilt about their senseless deaths would haunt him forever.

There was no other explanation behind Megan's disappearance. And he was to blame for it. *Vengeance,* the emails had read. Guilt filtered through every fiber in his body. All he could do was thump his fists against the wall in anger.

He needed to calm down, confide in someone he trusted. He called Dan Cummings, a Toronto lawyer and close friend who'd been at his side through the ups and downs of his life more than anyone else. Michael had almost chosen the legal profession as a career path, but then he realized he had a better chance of nabbing the bad guys if he didn't have to sift through piles of paperwork to do it.

A voice recording indicated that Dan was out of town at a lawyers' conference. Michael left a message anyway.

His phone buzzed seconds later. It was Kayla from Bradford Publishing.

He'd forgotten he'd left her a message about Megan's eight o'clock meeting with a client last night.

"Sorry about not returning your call until now," Kayla said, concern running through her voice. "The police left me a message too, but I decided to call you first. Has something happened to Megan?"

"I was hoping you could tell me," Michael snapped.

"What?" Kayla's voice rose in pitch.

He caught himself. "Sorry, Kayla. I didn't mean to be rude. Megan is missing. I filed a report with the police last night."

She drew in a quick breath. "Oh, no! It explains why she didn't show up at Bradford last night or answer my phone calls."

"Did she call her client?"

"I don't think so. A staff member sat with the client in our boardroom last night while she tried to reach Megan. The client finally left. This isn't like Megan at all."

"I know." What else could he say?

Kayla broke the silence after what seemed like an eternity. "Don't worry about Megan's work projects. I'll cover for her. If it's not too much trouble, Michael, please keep me posted if you hear from her."

That her co-workers cared about Megan gave him some comfort. "Sure."

Michael moved to the ensuite and took a shower. He let the warm water pulse against his aching neck while he planned his next move. He needed to relax and remain objective. As detached as it sounded, the only way he would succeed in finding Megan was to treat her disappearance like one of the other investigative cases he'd handled. Emotions had to take a back seat. Logic would dictate every step he took from now on.

Next he called Esposito to find out if he'd made any headway after interviewing the nanny this morning. If Megan had met with another real estate agent on Parkhurst Street in broad daylight, someone had to have seen her.

Michael had another, more justifiable, reason for wanting to speak with Esposito. Although he'd searched the condo as the detective had suggested, he hadn't bought his excuse about Megan leaving him. Sure, he felt responsible for her disappearance, but not for the absurd reason Esposito had insinuated.

The threatening messages on Michael's phone were proof that outside factors were at play.

The detective didn't pick up, so Michael left a message. All the better. He needed time to chill out completely before he spoke with him.

Michael had avoided calling Megan's mother last night to tell her about his visit with Esposito. He kept hoping the front door would open and Megan would walk in with a plausible excuse—even if it were the middle of the night.

It was time now. He reached for his phone and called her.

"Did Megan come back home?" was the first thing Connie asked him.

He brought her up to date and kept her hopes high about potential leads. "They won't stop until they find her."

"Let's pray it's soon." Her voice was burdened with fatigue. "Tell me, Michael. Did you and Megan have an argument?"

He wished it was as simple as that. "No. We're good. Really we are." He anticipated her next question. "Megan didn't pack a bag and say she was leaving me or anything like that. It's the opposite. I don't know if she told you, but we're interested in buying a house. We recently went to showings in the area."

"Yes, she told me you wanted to buy a house nearby. I'm glad you're staying in the area." She paused, then quietly asked, "Michael, what do you think happened to Megan?"

He didn't want to cause Connie more stress by sharing his theories about retaliation from vindictive criminals. He opted for a reassuring approach instead. "The cops will be interviewing more people who might have seen her."

In a hushed voice, she asked, "Is it possible Megan was kidnapped?"

Her question exposed his deepest anxieties. Abductors usually contacted family members with a demand for ransom within the first twenty-four hours. He calmly said, "I don't know."

Connie let out a deep sigh. "I have to believe that Megan is okay...that she'll come back to us soon."

He wished he could say the same. As the hours passed, the odds of finding Megan alive diminished. He blocked out the ominous possibility. This wasn't just another case. It was about the woman he loved.

Yet he had to remain detached—no matter how close this investigation was to him. "If I hear anything at all, Connie, I promise I'll call you right away."

"Why don't you drop by? I'll be home all day."

"Sure. I'll see you later."

Next on his list was a call to his parents. He held the phone in his hand but hesitated. Previous conversations with his father had ended on a sour note. The topic was the same one they'd quarreled about for years: Michael's career path as an investigative journalist.

His father was semi-retired and wanted to hand the company reins over to someone he could trust—like his only child. But running his father's lucrative high-tech company wasn't where Michael's heart was. He hoped his father would understand one day. His mother had wisely stayed out of any disagreements between the two most important men in her life.

Right now, Michael needed to focus on finding Megan.

He called Derrick Ferguson, his boss at *The Gazette*. He told Derrick that he needed to take a few days off for personal reasons. He also requested more time to work on his article— the Hells Angels' trafficking of illegal opioids.

"I'll give you a week's extension," Derrick said.

"Thanks, that should do it." Michael choked on his words.

It didn't escape Derrick's attention. "What's wrong, Michael?"

"Uh...nothing."

"I'm not buying it. We've known each other for... How long? Five years? You know you can confide in me. What's the problem?"

Michael trusted Derrick. Having worked as a journalist half of his life, forty-five-year-old Derrick understood the demands of investigative reporting and its inherent risks. He'd confided in Michael when he'd struggled with an alcohol addiction that almost cost him his job and his marriage several years back. Michael had persuaded him to get the help he needed. The men had enjoyed a relationship built on mutual trust ever since.

"Megan is missing," Michael blurted.

"Missing? How? When?"

Michael brought him up to date.

"Oh, man, I'm so sorry," Derrick said. "Any leads?"

"Nothing from the cops so far. They asked me to come up with a list of potential kidnappers—like the guys I helped put behind bars."

"I feel your pain. Let me know if I can help you in any way. In the meantime, I'll keep my eyes and ears open for any trickles our reporters get from their informants. Some lowlife involved in Megan's kidnapping might brag about it to the wrong person. Talk to you later."

Derrick's comment about informants reminded Michael about his pub meeting at the other end of town. Could a ploy to detain him miles away from Megan have been part of the plan to kidnap her? He had to know for sure. One person might be able to dispel his doubts: Willie, one of his reliable informants. He put a call in to him and left a message.

Michael walked aimlessly back to the kitchen and stared at the bowl of fruit Megan had placed in the center of the table. She said the energy of fruits promoted good *feng shui*. He could definitely use more positive energy to help get his life back on track.

He opened the fridge, took note of the eggs and cheese, then changed his mind. He wasn't hungry. Normally a healthy eater, he blamed guilty feelings about Megan's disappearance for his abrupt loss of appetite.

Smarten up, he told himself. You can't run on empty.

He opened the fridge again and took out two eggs, then prepared an omelet topped with shredded mozzarella cheese. He brewed a pot of his favorite Colombian coffee and had a cup while he plotted his next move.

But self-doubts trickled through. Maybe Esposito was right, and he should stay out of it. Did he really have what it took to remain objective in his search for Megan? Or would he provoke anyone who looked at him sideways?

Michael couldn't deny he'd rubbed a lot of people the wrong way. From heartless killers to shrewd fraudsters, they'd threatened to take him down, one way or another. It was a long shot to think he could identify Megan's abductor without taking precise and calculated steps to get there. Even narrowing his list of suspects to a handful was a challenging task in itself.

And then what? He couldn't go it alone. He needed help. Esposito's help.

Before he headed out to meet with the detective, he changed into a clean shirt and beige khakis. He had slipped into his leather jacket and was about to leave when the doorbell rang. He hit the intercom button. It was Esposito.

He broke into a cold sweat. If Esposito had come here to talk to him in person, it could only mean one thing: He had news.

Bad news.

9

———

MICHAEL

Wednesday morning

"No, she hasn't come back home," Michael said in response to Esposito's question about Megan. He led the detective into the living room and sat on the sofa by the window. "Any news at your end?"

Esposito settled in an adjacent armchair. He pulled out a black notebook from his suit pocket and flipped through the pages. "I spoke with Kayla at Bradford Publishing."

Michael had already received the inside scoop directly from Kayla, but he let Esposito finish on the off chance he'd picked up more information.

"Megan was a no-show for a client meeting there last night," the detective said. "The staff had no contact with her by phone either."

"Which means she disappeared long before then," Michael pointed out.

"It's a safe assumption." Esposito flipped to the next page. "I already mentioned Brett Paquette at MRG and how Megan called him to cancel the Hillside Avenue showing last evening."

"She *called* him? You didn't mention that before."

Esposito peered at his notes. "My mistake. She sent him a text message to cancel and said you would reschedule."

"I don't buy it. Megan would have called me if she couldn't make it. Her kidnapper could have sent that message."

The detective nodded in agreement. "If she was kidnapped, anything's possible."

"Any leads on her car?"

"Not yet." Esposito glanced at his notes. "I returned to the house on Parkhurst Street this morning. The nanny confirmed she saw a woman fitting Megan's description get out of a car and meet a man in front of the house around six o'clock last evening. There was a brief exchange and they drove off in their separate cars."

"Did she get a description of the guy?"

"He was tall with a muscular build, had brown hair, and wore sunglasses."

"That's it?"

"He wore a dark jacket and beige khakis." Inadvertently or not, his eyes swept over Michael's attire.

"It wasn't me. You already know I have an alibi. Besides, lots of guys fit that description."

The detective shrugged. "You have to admit it's quite the coincidence, isn't it?"

Michael ignored the implication. "Did the nanny hear what Megan and the guy were talking about?"

"No. She noticed something else, though." He tapped his notebook. "This is where it gets dicey."

"Dicey? How?"

"He handed Megan a bouquet of flowers."

Michael felt as if someone had punched him in the gut. And here he was, getting ready to quash the detective's theory about Megan leaving him. "She's not having an affair, so let's not even go there."

But Esposito persisted. "The man gave her flowers. It's odd

for a real estate agent to do that. Don't you think?"

Despite the perceived setback of this recent revelation, Michael maintained his composure. "I want to show you a notation that validates Megan's meeting last night. I'll go get it." He headed for Megan's office and returned with her agenda. He showed Esposito the note she'd scribbled about the house showing on Parkhurst Street at six o'clock. "It looks like she scheduled a meeting with another real estate agent. Maybe she didn't tell me about it because she knew I couldn't go. Or maybe she wanted to surprise me."

Esposito dug out his phone and took a photo of the page. "It was a viable lead until I interviewed the people at that address." He tucked his phone away.

"What do you mean?" Michael placed Megan's agenda on the coffee table and sat back down. It was clear the detective wasn't going to let his suspicions about him dissipate that easily. Or was this about something else?

"The Parkhurst home wasn't for sale. Something else might be going on in Megan's life that you don't know about." The detective waited for a reaction.

"Like I told you, our relationship is in excellent shape. And by the way, nothing belonging to Megan is missing here. No clothes, no luggage, nothing. Megan is cautious. She wouldn't have met with the guy for a showing without checking him out before. She was convinced he was okay."

Esposito raised a hand. "Before we jump to conclusions, let's get one thing straight. Whoever this mystery man is, he might not be linked to Megan's disappearance. Something could have happened to her *after* their meeting."

"He's still a lead in my books. The sooner we find him, the sooner we find Megan."

"I agree he's a potential lead, but we have to explore the evidence further."

"What evidence?"

"I've requested a copy of the home security video from the

owners on Parkhurst Street. It might help us to identify the mystery man and his vehicle."

"Right." Michael held back from saying how he couldn't wait to get his hands on the jerk, but he kept his cool for the detective's sake. The video would also reveal what Megan was wearing that day, and that subject would be put to rest.

Esposito went on. "In the event that this mystery man turns out to be legitimate and without reproach, do you know anyone else who might have wished Megan harm?"

"No."

"Would anyone want to target you through Megan? You did say that every investigative reporter has enemies."

Michael nodded. "You know how it works. You help put someone in jail. Next thing you hear, there's a contract out on your life."

"Whoever is behind Megan's disappearance might have sent you those threatening messages."

"True. I've been getting threats for years, but I didn't take them seriously until now."

"I meant to ask you this earlier." Esposito gave him a measured look. "You and Megan are shopping for a home in an exclusive area of town. How does a crime reporter's salary begin to cover the mortgage on a luxury house?"

"What are you getting at?"

"The home you're interested in buying is a major leap in price from your condo."

Michael grinned. Esposito had done a recent background search on him. "I didn't know it was a crime to buy a more expensive home."

"Indulge me anyway."

He hated to disclose personal information, but under the circumstances, he had no choice. "The proceeds from the sale of our condo will go toward the purchase of the new place. I also inherited a substantial sum from my late grandmother. And I have a trust fund my parents set up for me."

"A trust fund? How much are we talking?"

"In the seven figures."

The detective blinked. "So your parents come from a family of considerable means."

"Their money isn't my money," Michael snapped. "But since you apparently have me on your suspect list—"

Esposito raised his hands. "Relax, Michael. I'm looking for a viable motive behind Megan's disappearance. That's all."

"You have a strange way of getting at it."

The detective shifted in his chair. "Then I'll be blunt. Has anyone contacted you for a ransom?"

"No, but I'd rather get a call. It would be a lot better than facing the alternative."

"I agree." He flipped to another page in his notebook. "You mentioned yesterday that you had a list of potential suspects."

"I have a handful of contenders. As far as I know, they're still serving time."

"It doesn't matter. They could have far-reaching tentacles to the outside."

"I'm aware of that."

"Can you give me their names and brief details on their criminal history?"

"No problem. I'll prepare a list for you today."

"Good." Esposito put away his notebook and stood up. "I'll keep in touch."

After the detective left, Michael placed a call. It was the first step in his plan to find Megan. His tactics would involve detailed work that no police force would have the time or manpower to carry out. After he'd achieved specific objectives, he would bring Esposito on board to help him follow through to the end.

Since the detective didn't seem to trust him completely, there was no way in hell he was going to share his strategies with him just yet.

10

___

MEGAN

Wednesday morning

Loud voices woke me up.

It was dark. I was confused, until I remembered I was in someone's dusty, unfinished basement.

My hands were cold and shackled behind me. My feet were in chains. I forced myself up to a sitting position and listened.

A shaft of light hit the floor at the foot of the staircase. Someone had opened the door leading down here.

"I'll be back by noon," a woman's raspy voice reached me. "You watch her like a hawk, Lardo. You hear me?"

"Aw, do I have to stay down there?" Lardo whined. "She's all tied up. She's not goin' anywhere like that."

"The boss said you have to stay in the basement."

"But I want to sit on a couch like you do. It's hard to sit on a metal chair all day."

"Just do it, if you know what's good for you!"

"Where are you goin'?"

"None of your business." The woman's heels tapped across the foyer. The front door slammed shut behind her.

A car engine revved. It didn't sound like my car. With the police on the lookout for it, Lardo and the woman had surely disposed of it by now.

Lardo's heavy footsteps sounded on the basement stairs. He rounded the corner with a breakfast tray and came up to me.

The contents included a cup with no more than several ounces of coffee and a slice of burnt toast—no butter.

My stomach growled and my head ached. When was the last time I'd eaten a full meal? They were evidently trying to starve me to death.

"I put a cube of sugar in your coffee." Lardo grinned. "Don't tell anyone—especially Tiny. She'll get real mad." His lips twisted in a grimace.

Tiny? Was that her name? How peculiar that nothing would frighten Lardo more than a loudmouthed woman with a diminutive name and a mean attitude. I smiled inwardly at the irony of it all.

Lardo ripped the pieces of tape off my mouth.

I cried out in agony, certain that he'd pulled off a layer of skin too.

"Sorry." He unlocked my handcuffs, then sat in front of the TV while I drank my coffee and ate my toast. "Now don't yell and get me in trouble again, or I'll have to put the tape back."

We'd developed a silent understanding between us since yesterday. If I didn't scream, he wouldn't punch me out. If I didn't ask him questions or talk too much, he'd let me finish my meal. Reasonable enough.

"Wanna watch TV?" Lardo asked me. "I can turn it around so you can see it better."

"Okay," I said, keeping my words to a minimum.

The TV show was a rerun of *ALF*, an eighties sitcom about an alien entity who crash lands in the garage of a suburban middle-class family. Lardo found it humorous. Maybe his roaring guffaws were loud enough to alert the neighbors.

But as time went by, no such luck.

I pretended to watch TV all morning, but my focus was elsewhere. I needed to convince Lardo to bring me upstairs.

As the show ended, Lardo turned to me. "You finished eating?"

"Yes," I said, "but I need to go to the bathroom."

"You have to stay down here."

"Is there a toilet in the basement?"

"No. Only upstairs."

"We can go upstairs. I won't tell anyone, I promise."

Lardo pondered his decision. "Uh...okay." He bent down to unfasten the chains around my feet, then clasped my arm as we climbed the stairs. He led me to the bathroom on the first floor. "Go. Be quick in case Tiny comes back."

I lost no time. I peered inside the cabinets under the sink to see if something might serve as a weapon. They were empty, except for rolls of toilet paper. Nothing on the counter except a soap dispenser and a hand towel. The room had a window, but security bars on the outside discouraged any notion of trying to escape through there.

After we returned to the basement, Lardo handcuffed me and gently put the pieces of tape back over my mouth. I caught a flicker of concern in his eyes. Was I imagining it?

I hoped not. A friend would come in handy right now.

Since Lardo seldom stopped on a TV channel that indicated the time, I counted the passage of hours by the number of programs he watched. Each sitcom ran half an hour. Each movie, about one and a half hours—depending on the number of commercials included. The total for this morning after he'd watched three sitcoms and a movie? Three hours.

My stomach made gurgling noises that sounded like a baby crying out for nourishment. I desperately craved an apple...a piece of cheese...chocolate almonds...anything!

With Lardo's consistent appetite, I didn't have to worry about missing a meal—if you could describe the slim pickings they served me as that. According to my calculations, it was noon and time for him to head upstairs and fetch a food tray from the kitchen.

I couldn't visualize Lardo concocting meals in the kitchen, nor would I feel comfortable ingesting anything his grubby hands touched. My only consolation was that, sooner rather than later, he'd go upstairs in search of food.

I jumped as a petite blonde-haired woman stepped into the basement. The blaring TV had masked the sound of her foot-steps on the stairs.

Hands on her hips, her spiky metal heels firmly planted on the cement floor, she stared at Lardo. "Turn off that blasted TV!"

I recognized her throaty voice. It was Tiny. Strangely enough, she seemed familiar, but I couldn't place her.

Lardo rose to his feet, knocking over his chair. "Tiny, you're back. I didn't hear you come downstairs." He did as he was told, then folded the chair and placed it against the wall.

Tiny perused the food trays scattered here and there. "It looks like a friggin' pigsty down here." She wrinkled her nose and waved a hand in front of her thin face. "It stinks like one too. The boss won't stand for this one bit. Go get a garbage bag upstairs and bring down the tray of food I left on the counter."

As Lardo bolted past her and up the stairs, I contemplated how such a small woman could wield so much power over a big hulk like him.

And who was this boss they kept referring to?

Tiny took out a pack of cigarettes from her shoulder bag. She lit one and blew a puff of smoke in the air.

I suddenly remembered where I'd seen her before. She'd attended the so-called home showing on Parkvale Street.

Were we still in the same house?

Ken had said a relative was holding the home showing. Was Tiny that relative?

What did she want from me?

So many questions.

Tiny eyed me with contempt. "I know you've been talking to Lardo...asking him about Ken, the real estate agent. Forget it. You'll never see him again." She puffed on her cigarette.

What did they do to Ken? Did they kill him?

She strutted up to me, the needle marks on her arms a sign she was a drug user. "It won't be long now," she sneered.

What did she mean by that? Were they planning to get rid of me too?

Tiny drew another puff and blew it in my direction.

I turned away. With my mouth taped up, the last thing I needed was to inhale smoke and cough to death.

She took two more puffs, then dropped the cigarette stub and ground it with her shoe. She turned toward the stairs and bellowed, "What are you doing up there, Lardo?"

He replied, but I couldn't make out what he said.

"Whatever." Tiny pulled out her phone and tapped a few buttons. "Hi, it's Tiny. Yeah, it's a new phone... Really?" She laughed. "I knew it would make your day... Yeah, a real surprise reunion. No, she wasn't interested in the house after all. Yeah, too bad." She grinned at me, then put on a fake pout.

She was talking about me!

Tiny paced back and forth, her heels clicking against the cement floor. "Okay, but we'll have to wait till later for that," she said into the phone. "I called you because I'm going out of town for a while and—" She laughed again. "You know me so well. Meet you at the usual place? Okay. Two o'clock." She ended the call.

Lardo hurried down the stairs, a large garbage bag folded over his shoulder, a tray of food in his hands.

"It's about time," Tiny said to him. "Don't forget. After you're done, throw out the leftovers. Bring the empty plates and trays upstairs to the kitchen. Don't leave anything around down here. Not a damn thing. You got it?"

"Got it," Lardo said. He set the tray on the floor, then placed a bowl before me.

The minuscule bowl of noodle soup and two wrapped soda crackers were disheartening. But I had a utensil this time—a soupspoon. If they were feeding me only enough to keep me alive, they had an endgame in mind. But what was it?

In comparison with my meager spread, Lardo's lunch was an enormous bowl of soup and a three-decker salami sandwich. The odor from the latter filled the air, overpowering even Lardo's personal scent.

"Don't forget," Tiny said to him. "No snacks for her. Got it?"

"Got it."

"I'll be leaving in a couple of hours."

"Where are you goin', Tiny?"

"Out."

"Where?" he repeated.

"Again, none of your business." She headed for the stairs.

Lardo's eyes narrowed. After Tiny had turned the corner and mounted the stairs, he remained there, staring, fists opening and closing at his side, as if he were imagining a physical retaliation of sorts. Grumbling under his breath, he turned and began to clean up. He emptied the plates of leftover food, stacked them onto the trays, and carried the whole lot upstairs. With twisted amusement, I noticed he'd left the garbage bag in the basement by the stairs—probably to avoid another outburst from Tiny after the next meal.

The obvious friction between those two was something I planned to take advantage of. Divide and conquer, as the saying went. All I needed was the right opportunity.

On his return, Lardo removed the tape from my mouth and unshackled my hands. "Eat." He pointed to my bowl of soup. "You have to eat." After sitting down to enjoy his own meal, he turned on the TV, changed the channel to a game show, and raised the volume.

Managing my every move gave Lardo a sense of purpose or control—something Tiny managed to strip from him every time she demeaned his behavior. Yes, there was no love lost between those two.

I didn't have much to eat, but I made sure to drink a spoonful of soup and take a bite of my cracker every time Lardo looked my way. I didn't have to go through the motions for much longer. He soon became so engrossed in the game show that his attention remained glued to the screen.

The boisterous chimes and cheers from the TV audience worked to my advantage. They cloaked the grating sound my spoon made as I scooped up bits of cement dust and insects— and anything else that came along for the ride—near the unfinished wall beside me. I discreetly dumped the contents into my bowl and stirred. I crushed the other cracker to provide more consistency to my soup and camouflage its contents, then launched my plan into action during a commercial break.

"I'm not hungry," I said.

Lardo gaped at me. "Huh?"

"I don't want the soup," I shouted over the noisy TV.

He placed his empty plate on the tray. "You sure?" He gawked at my bowl and licked his lips.

"Yes."

He grabbed my bowl and proceeded to eat. After the first spoonful, he said, "You shouldn't have put crackers in here. It makes it taste like chalk."

I held my breath and said nothing.

After he finished the soup, Lardo let out an enormous burp. He placed a hand on his stomach and said, "I don't feel so good." He turned off the TV, bounded from the chair, and scrambled up the stairs.

Repulsive sounds of Lardo vomiting, then flushing the toilet in the first-floor bathroom, carried down to the basement.

Tiny's heels clacked as she crossed the foyer. She closed the bathroom door to block out the disgusting sounds, if not to give Lardo some privacy.

"What the hell have you been eating now, Lardo?" Tiny shouted. "You can't fool me. I know you've been stealing all kinds of food from the pantry."

My plan had worked. All I had to do was wait for the animosity to flare up between them.

I wanted to believe that Lardo and I had formed a bond of trust from sharing time and space with each other. Because of that trust, he'd given me a degree of freedom. Which would explain why I was sitting here—not gagged, hands untied, and a lethal soupspoon tucked in a side pocket of my pants. I hadn't felt this secure since the day before they'd kidnapped me.

But it was wishful thinking on my part. Lardo had simply rushed off to empty his guts. He would be back soon.

The doorbell rang.

My heart beat faster.

"Who the hell could that be?" Tiny's heels clicked rapidly across the ceramic floor. In her hurry, she didn't close the door leading to the basement.

"Hello, I live in the house next door," a woman's frail voice drifted in. "Would you have a moment?"

"What do you want?" Tiny asked, clearly annoyed.

"I was wondering if I might ask you a question about—"

I didn't catch the rest of her sentence. Nor did I want to. It was now or never.

I screamed as loud as I could.

A dog barked.

I screamed again.

Tiny said something I couldn't hear.

The front door slammed shut.

Heels clattered across the foyer and down the stairs.

I was in big trouble.

11

———

MEGAN

Wednesday afternoon

Fury blazed in Tiny's eyes as she flew across the basement floor and lunged at me, thrusting me onto my back. "You scheming tramp!" She clasped my neck and squeezed. "I'll give you something to scream about!"

I struggled to pry her bony fingers from my neck. She was surprisingly strong for an underweight druggie. I couldn't break her grasp.

The spoon was in my back pocket, but I couldn't reach for it. I was too busy preventing those powerful fingers from cutting off my air passage.

I was choking.

My vision was fading.

I was losing consciousness.

Tiny's legs jerked above me as Lardo snatched her away and broke her hold on me.

I bent over and gasped for air.

"You crazy or somethin'?" Lardo shouted at Tiny. "You almost killed her."

Tiny pointed at him. "The next time you touch me, Lardo, I promise you it'll be the last." She adjusted her T-shirt over her jeans.

"That makes twice you tried to kill her," Lardo said. "I'm gonna tell the boss what you did."

Tiny glared at him. "What are you talking about?"

"You put somethin' bad in her bowl of soup. You tried to poison her. The boss said we have to keep her alive."

Tiny's expression soured. "You're one big sicko, you know that? If you were doing your job instead of feeding your fat face in the kitchen whenever my back was turned, I wouldn't have to deal with that nosy neighbor again. Her dog heard this one screaming at the top of her lungs. I had to tell the old lady something about the TV being on too loud, then I shut the door in her face."

Lardo scowled at me. "I heard you screamin' too."

Tiny was relentless. "Just do your friggin' job, Lardo. That nosy neighbor might call the cops the next time. Then where would we be?"

Lardo groaned. "Why is it always my fault? I didn't do nothin'."

"Shut your mouth. If I hadn't asked the boss to hire you, you'd still be walking the streets, picking through garbage bins looking for your next meal. You're useless."

"Don't say that, Tiny. I helped you. I protected you when you bought your drugs from those scary dealers."

"I told you to shut up, Lardo! As for you..." She slapped me hard across the face. "If we hadn't been told to keep you alive, you'd be dead by now."

My cheek stung with pain. My vision blurred. I tasted blood and leaned over to spit it out.

Who was their boss?

Why did they have to keep me alive?

Tiny's attention strayed to the side pocket of my pants. "What's that?" She yanked out the spoon and waved it at Lardo.

"This is how you watch her?" She flung the spoon at him. It bounced off his stomach and hit the floor.

Lardo stood there, fists tightening, but he said nothing.

Tiny gestured toward me. "Bring her to the bathroom on the second floor and get her cleaned up. We don't want the boss to see her like this. It'll take away all the fun."

Fun?

She ranted on. "And make sure there's nothing in the bathroom that she could use as a weapon. Don't screw up this time. I have to go out."

"Again?" Lardo said.

"Yes."

"How come you get to go out and do all the cool stuff?"

"First, because I need to buy a supply of burner phones. Second, because I'm smarter than you." She sneered at him, then turned and hurried toward the stairs.

Lardo grimaced at her back. He waited until she reached the top of the stairs, then said to me, "I won't tie you up. Don't try nothin' stupid, okay? I don't want to hurt you."

"Okay." I stood up. My legs were a little wobbly. I reached out to put a hand on his arm to steady myself.

"You go ahead. If you fall, I can catch you."

His consideration didn't surprise me. After all, we had something in common. We were both victims of Tiny's spiteful abuse—verbal and physical.

As we stepped into the foyer, the front door shut. With Tiny gone, had the odds of escaping from here just improved?

Lardo grabbed my arm before I could react and led me up another flight of stairs to the bathroom. He looked inside the cabinets under the sink and peeked behind the shower curtain. Satisfied that no lethal weapons were at my disposal, he stepped out and closed the door behind him.

Alone, I went through the same motions as Lardo. There was nothing in the cabinets except a pile of towels, rolls of toilet paper, and personal toiletries. As in the main floor bathroom, a soap dispenser and a hand towel sat on the counter.

Why did Tiny insinuate that there might be a potential weapon in here?

I ran the cold water in the sink and drank from the tap until I quenched my thirst. I switched to hot water and washed my hands and face, taking note of the red marks around my neck—Tiny's imprints. I let the hot water run until it steamed up the mirror, then traced my initials and left a thumbprint in a lower corner. If we left this place before the police found me, the evidence would let them know I was here. I quickly fanned the air with the towel to dissipate the steam.

My eyes flitted around the bathroom again. The chance of finding something I could use as a weapon was close to nil.

Almost.

The shower curtain had retro mirror hooks. If I removed one and bunched the curtain, no one would notice it was missing. I touched the inside of the bathtub. It was dry, which told me none of my kidnappers had taken a shower here recently.

A knock sounded at the door.

"Hurry up in there!" Lardo said.

I flushed the toilet and removed one of the curtain hooks. The noise from the toilet hid the sound of the hooks sliding along the metal rod as I gathered the curtain. I slipped the hook inside the pocket of my pants and opened the door.

Lardo stood there, his arms folded in a show of impatience. "What took you so long?"

One glance at him and I dismissed any notion of trying to escape. I wouldn't make it out the front door, let alone down the stairs to the foyer, with that Goliath shadowing me. "I'm a woman," I said, improvising. "These things take time."

He stared at me, confused.

Back in the basement, I stretched my arms out before me. Maybe Lardo wouldn't notice that I hadn't extended them behind my back.

He didn't. After he shackled my feet, he didn't put the tape back over my mouth. He simply sauntered off to his usual post in front of the TV.

I'd become invisible again.

Apprehension trickled along my spine. Would I ever get out of here?

12
———

MICHAEL

Wednesday afternoon

To initiate his search for Megan and her kidnapper, Michael would need help from trustworthy people. He set up a time to meet with Derrick at *The Gazette* later, then called Brett Paquette at MRG to say he was driving over right away.

"I cleared my schedule as soon as you called," Brett said. He ushered Michael along a corridor bordering an open-concept nest of offices and into one of the private conference rooms. "Any news on Megan?"

"Nothing yet," Michael said.

"Sorry to hear that. Please, have a seat." Brett motioned toward a couple of empty chairs. "What can I do for you?"

Michael trusted Brett but nevertheless chose to tread lightly and not reveal all his cards. "Megan was seen with a man in front of a Parkhurst Street address before she disappeared. There's a possibility he was a real estate agent."

Brett passed a hand over his tie. "It wasn't me. I already told you she canceled our appointment for the showing on Hillside Avenue. I don't know what she did afterward."

"Would a colleague from MRG have suggested another home showing to her yesterday?"

"I have no idea. What are you getting at, Michael?"

"Do you know if another agent at MRG has a listing on Parkhurst Street?"

"Let me check the MLS." Brett moved over to a computer on the table and accessed the website. "What's the address?"

Michael gave it to him.

"It's not listed on the MLS."

"What about an agent listing from another real estate company?"

Brett shrugged. "Same story. All agent listings would show up on the MLS."

"An agent might have invited Megan to a private showing— the way you did for the house on Hillside Avenue."

"Maybe. The owners there wanted me to cherry-pick visitors for the showings. They refused to have just anyone walk off the street and into their home. There's one problem with a private showing, though."

"What's that?"

"When a property is up for a private sale, it's not listed on the MLS, so not many people know about it."

Michael persisted. "What about other recently listed houses in the area that fit the description and price range we're asking for?"

"You're in luck. I gather that kind of data for market comparisons, so I have the latest information on hand. Let's go back to my desk."

Michael followed Brett through the cluster of offices. There were eight desks, but only two other agents were present: a middle-aged woman who was speaking on the phone and a tall, dark-haired guy in a suit that would have cost Michael a month's salary.

Brett pulled out a chair at his desk. "Have a seat, Michael." He reached for another chair and sat down in front of his computer. "Let's see what we have."

Michael looked on as Brett studied the files on his desktop.

"Here it is." Brett clicked open a file. The screen displayed photos of two-story houses. "These are the homes on the market that include most of the features you specified. Their respective addresses are listed below the photos."

As Michael examined them, he recognized most of the homes he and Megan had visited.

Just then the dark-haired agent in the expensive suit came up to Brett. "Sorry to interrupt. I need your witness signature on these documents." He held out a folder.

"Can't it wait a few minutes, Ken?"

"Not really. I'm meeting with the client soon."

While Brett signed the documents, Ken openly stared at the information on his computer screen. The guy had no scruples, Michael thought.

Brett handed the folder back to Ken, who thanked him and returned to his desk. "Aside from the homes you and Megan visited with me," he said to Michael, "no new listings have been added in the last week. It's basically a seller's market."

Michael was half-listening. His attention had remained on Ken who now picked up his briefcase and rushed off. He kept his voice low. "Brett, is your colleague usually that nosy?"

"What do you mean?"

"He was gawking at your computer screen while you were signing his papers."

Brett scanned the floor to make sure the agent had left, then whispered, "That was Ken Reilly. If there's one thing I can't stand, it's an agent who tries to steal my clients."

"How?"

"There are lots of ways. Here's an example. They find out about other agents' open house showings, then stand outside and hand out their business cards to prospective clients going in or coming out of the house. Ken was probably scouting out my prospects."

"You're kidding," Michael said. "Isn't that unethical?"

"Sort of. Here's how it's supposed to work. If another agent has an interested buyer for my client's house, he would approach me first. Realtors' ethical standards are strict about things like that."

"Can't they do anything about agents who steal clients?"

"They'll investigate complaints, but if the house isn't on the MLS, they can't do a thing about it. There's no exclusive agreement in place."

"Sounds like a losing proposition for the agents who follow the rules. It must be tough to protect your interests."

"It's easy to overhear conversations in this place," Brett said. "We sit a couple of feet away from one another. That's why I work from home most of the time. Privacy concerns."

A theory began to form in Michael's mind. It didn't take a math course to deduce that another MRG agent could have overheard Brett's side of the conversation with him about the house showing on Hillside Avenue. Or even spied over Brett's shoulder to collect the names of potential buyers—like Ken Reilly did.

Now that he'd seen Ken in action, Michael had more than a fleeting curiosity in him. That the guy was about his height and build hadn't escaped his attention either. He'd try to find out more about him.

But first, he had to make two other stops.

For every investigative venture Michael undertook, he let his instincts guide him and his willpower propel him forward. Megan's disappearance merited a tenfold effort in those aspects.

He was determined to knock on every door in the Parkhurst Street neighborhood if he needed to. Aside from the nanny, someone else must have noticed Megan and the kidnapper who lured her away. Damn him!

Control your impulses, he reminded himself. Angry talk won't get you anywhere. Stay cool.

He drove slowly past the house on Parkhurst Street where the nanny claimed to have seen Megan. He circled the block and spotted only one For Sale sign on the front lawn of a luxurious home, confirming what Brett had told him about the scarcity of houses for sale in the area.

He extended his drive to a two-block radius and stopped to speak with a middle-aged man who was mowing the front lawn. He showed him Megan's photo, but the man hadn't seen her.

Negative replies didn't discourage Michael. He stretched his drive to a three-block radius. The houses here were older and larger—well above the price range that he and Megan had planned for.

He spotted an elderly woman with a cane. She was walking a beige cocker spaniel on a leash. He stepped out of the car and went through the same routine with the photo, asking if she'd seen Megan.

"She's a lovely girl," the woman said, smiling. "No, I haven't seen her. Has she gone missing?"

"Yes," Michael said.

"What a coincidence. Helen, my next-door neighbor, has gone missing too."

Michael's pulse picked up speed. Another kidnapping in the area? "Recently?"

"Yes, this week. It's most peculiar. We used to chat every morning when we watered our flower gardens, but I haven't seen her the past couple of days."

"Maybe she's ill," he said, deferring to logic.

"I doubt it. Yesterday I knocked on her door. A young woman answered and said she was housekeeping while Helen was away on a trip. It's quite peculiar."

"What's peculiar?"

"Helen is eighty years old and lives alone. I doubt that she'd leave on a trip without telling me. She has trouble getting around and uses a cane like this one." She tapped the sidewalk with hers.

The dog barked.

"Oh, hush up, Ginger." She turned to Michael. "She only barks when someone knocks on the front door or rings the doorbell. I'm hearing-impaired, you see."

Michael listened politely, but he had no time for idle chatter. He was about to offer an excuse to leave when the woman went on.

"You know, Ginger has been barking a lot at Helen's house for no reason lately. She lives over there." She nodded toward the two-story century-old brick home over her right shoulder. "My name is Dorothy, by the way. I live next door." She pointed to a similar red brick structure over her left shoulder.

"Impressive homes."

"Yes, they definitely are," Dorothy said. "To finish my story, I knocked on Helen's door again today to ask the housekeeper if she had any news from my friend. She said no. When Ginger started to bark, the housekeeper said something about the TV being on too loud. Then she practically shut the door in my face. Quite rude, if not peculiar all the same."

Michael's guard was up. "Would you like me to take a look around?"

"Yes, if you wouldn't mind. I have to say I'm quite worried about Helen. Maybe you'll have better luck." She ambled along the sidewalk with him until they reached her neighbor's house.

With no fencing separating the two properties, Michael strode along the grass between the houses until he reached a window at the basement level in Helen's home. He peered inside, but drawn curtains prevented him from seeing anything. He rounded the front corner of the house and looked upward. The curtains were drawn on all the windows—a sign that Helen might be away.

He climbed the flight of stairs leading to the front door and rang the bell, waited, then knocked. No one answered. Either Helen wasn't at home as the housekeeper had said or she was incapacitated somehow.

Not wanting to alarm Dorothy, he walked back to her and said, "If you're worried about your neighbor, you can call the cops and ask them to come by. They might even be able to contact Helen's next of kin to verify her whereabouts."

"That's a wonderful idea," Dorothy said. "Thank you. You've been so helpful."

"If you happen to talk to Helen, would you ask her if she's seen Megan? Here's my business card."

She took the card. "Oh, I remember something else. Helen had the painters over this week to do some work in her basement. I've used them before. They're superb. Anyway, I haven't seen them lately either." Her brow furrowed. "I suppose Helen thought her trip was more important."

Michael returned to his car. The next person on his visitor list was Megan's mother. How could he keep her hopes high while preparing her for the worst possible outcome?

13

———

MICHAEL

Wednesday afternoon

The dark bags under Connie's eyes were a telltale sign that she was losing sleep over her daughter's disappearance. No sooner had she ushered Michael inside her condo apartment than she bombarded him with questions. "What did the police say? Did they find out anything more about Megan?"

"They're reviewing a security video from the area where she was last seen," Michael said, removing his jacket. "A witness told the cops that Megan met a man outside a home where a showing was supposed to take place. She seemed to know him." He choked up, cleared his throat. He couldn't tell her that a more intricate plot might be behind Megan's disappearance.

"A man? Do they know who he is?" Connie hung up his jacket in the closet, then led him down the hallway and into the kitchen.

"No." Michael pulled out a chair at the table and sat down. He was comfortable on visits here and attributed it to the warmth and generosity that Connie had shown him from the start. Their mutual love for Megan cemented their strong bond.

Connie wrung her hands. "What about Megan's car?"

He took a deep breath. There was no way around the truth. "They haven't found her car yet."

Tears welled in her eyes, and she hastened to the stove where she took the lid off two pots. "I've been cooking. It helps to calm my nerves and pass the time. It makes me feel like I'm doing something useful. I hope you're hungry." She set a plate of pasta and meatballs on the table before him.

"Thank you. It looks great."

She reached for a basket of fresh-cut bread on the counter and placed it on the table, then sat down across from him.

"Aren't you eating?" he asked her.

"Oh, I ate earlier." She unfolded and folded the cotton napkin before her and smoothed out a non-existent wrinkle.

Michael sensed she hadn't eaten much of anything.

He felt guilty. It wasn't fair to tell Connie that her daughter hadn't resurfaced, and then sit down and eat as if nothing horrific had happened. He took a few bites to please her, but even the scrumptious meal she'd prepared couldn't stir his appetite. It said a lot about the anxiety intensifying inside him.

Connie's forehead creased with worry lines. "You know, Megan wouldn't disappear for no reason. And she always calls me back when I leave her a message. Except for the last time." She paused. "Doesn't the police usually ask for help from the public regarding missing persons?"

Michael put down his fork. "They do. They're just trying to gather more information."

"More information? Don't they have a photo of Megan? A description of the clothes she was wearing?" Her eyes searched his, as if she believed he was the only person who could have provided such details to the police.

"Yes," he simply replied, too ashamed to admit he didn't know what Megan was wearing when she left the condo.

Though it wasn't the reason behind Esposito's delay in releasing a missing person report, he sensed the detective secretly faulted him for not providing that piece of information. The woman he loved was gone, and he couldn't even offer the cops the most basic of details—what she was wearing. At least the Parkhurst video would.

"You hardly touched your food," Connie said. "What's the matter? Don't you like it?"

Michael managed a brief smile. "It's delicious, but I don't have much of an appetite lately."

She patted his arm. "I understand. I feel the same way. It's hard to go on when we don't what happened to Megan. I try not to imagine the worst."

"She knows how to take care of herself," he said, trying to reassure her. Or maybe himself.

Connie fingered her wedding ring. She still wore the simple band of gold, even though her husband had passed away years ago. "Did you tell your parents about Megan?"

Her question caught him off guard. Megan had probably given her mother whatever background details she knew about his family—which wasn't much since he rarely mentioned them. "No, I haven't. I kept hoping Megan would show up."

"Family is important," she said softly. "They share your joys and your sorrows."

Megan had often mentioned how her Irish-Italian family members supported one another through difficult times. But he didn't want to bring up the subject of family right now—*his* family, that is. He'd burned too many bridges, and building new ones weren't his priority.

His phone rang. It was Willie, his informant. He wanted to meet with Michael immediately.

"I have to go," Michael said to Connie after he ended the call. "It's work related. Thanks for the pasta."

She touched his arm. "Michael, please promise me you'll find Megan."

He squeezed her hand. "I promise."

And he meant it.

Carrefour Laval mall bustled with activity and offered the perfect setting for Michael's meeting with Willie. Their conversation depended on secrecy, and loud music and noisy crowds worked as protective screens to that effect.

The two men strolled along the aisles housing the 150-store outlet. Better to be a moving target than a dead one, Willie had told him. To Michael's surprise, his Quebec informant had brushed up on his English recently. When he congratulated him on his achievement, Willie grinned, revealing a still-missing tooth on the right side of his mouth.

While Michael was eager to get answers to his questions, Willie insisted on sharing more news first. "I have other information that will interest you," he said, his words imbued with a French-Canadian accent. "It is about a member of the Hells Angels you helped put in a Quebec jail."

"Who?" Michael asked.

"Gabe Rivard. They released him this morning."

Michael stared at him. "Are you kidding? He got a ten-year sentence for illegal drug trafficking and operating prostitution rings last summer. Are you telling me he's already out?"

"It is not surprising." Willie adjusted his baseball cap. "The Hells Angels have the best lawyers working for them."

"Rivard must have struck a deal with the cops, given them the inside dope on gang operations."

"Misleading information." Willie chuckled. "If Rivard had told them the real facts, the bikers would have killed him the moment he walked out of jail."

"Where is he now?"

"I do not know. Listen, I have more to tell you. Remember that drug bust last year in Sainte-Adèle?"

"You bet I do." Michael had passed Willie's information along to the Quebec Provincial Police. "I rode with the QPP when they took down members of the Hells Angels."

"Other members started a new lab in the same area." Willie gave him a slip of paper. "It's already operational."

"Thanks." Michael tucked the note in his pocket. "By the way, would you know an informant named Raoul Levesque?"

Willie shook his head. "I never heard of him."

"Are you certain?"

"I know everyone who works underground. He is not one of us."

Michael grew silent. His suspicions that someone had purposefully sent him across town the other night was rapidly materializing into reality.

"Is something bothering you, Michael? You seem... What is the word? Moody."

Willie knew Megan. He'd met her during one of Michael's investigations years ago when she acted as a French translator for him. Since Michael trusted Willie, he told him about Megan's disappearance and how he could have been duped into meeting with an informant who might not exist.

Willie let out a string of swearwords in French. "I am sorry to hear that. If I find out anything, I will call you." He paused. "I do not mean to pour oil on the flame, as they say, but I have something else to tell you. Not only is Rivard a free man now, but he is also looking for *vengeance*."

Michael was surprised to hear a familiar word.

Willie went on. "The message on the street is that he wants to get even with *le journaliste anglais*. I think he means you."

Michael didn't doubt it. The evidence he'd gathered on the criminal operations of the Hells Angels over the years had helped put Gabe Rivard and other gang members behind bars. His ongoing investigative series for *The Gazette* had linked the gang's illegal drug-trafficking operations to the growing sale of synthetic opioids—like fentanyl—in which Rivard had played a critical part.

"It did not help that you mentioned Rivard by name in one of your articles, Michael."

"His name and jail term were already public knowledge by then."

"You know how gang members hate to be in the spotlight. They will do anything to avoid it."

Michael was adamant. "It's not going to stop me from warning the public about the hidden dangers of using street drugs. Thousands have died because they accidentally bought lethal drugs from dealers connected to the Hells Angels. The country is going through an opioid crisis. It's the least I can do to try to save lives."

"But the Hells Angels—"

"Tough luck. Someone has to flush out those rats."

"I agree," Willie said, "but there is a price to pay."

"You think Rivard went after Megan?"

"His anger has no boundaries. Megan is an easy target. You already know that these guys get even—one way or another."

"How can I find him?"

"You cannot," Willie said. "He is like a snake. He is an expert at hiding in plain sight. He will find you."

"Thanks for the heads-up." Michael slipped him a wad of twenty-dollar bills.

Willie gave him a wary look. "Watch your back, my friend."

14

MICHAEL

Wednesday afternoon

A vendetta against him. That was all Michael needed. Vengeance. Revenge. Retaliation. They all meant the same thing to him.

He'd checked his email an hour ago and found the message *vengeance* once again. It was useless to ask his tech friend to track down the source. Like the other messages he'd received, this one was probably sent from an anonymous location or a disposable phone. In essence, untraceable.

He sat down in the living room and opened up his laptop. He reviewed the list of suspects he'd prepared for Esposito. He wasn't naïve. He understood that these five suspects weren't the only perpetrators capable of kidnapping Megan.

Through his ongoing research into illegal drug-trafficking operations, he'd learned that several small-time thugs he'd helped to bring to justice were already back on the street peddling their wares. Any one of them with a score to settle could have shadowed Megan or him around town before deciding that Megan was an easier mark.

Constantly on his mind was the ongoing investigation into the Hells Angels. It had the potential to garner the wrong kind of attention from the wrong kind of people. Gang members preferred to spend their time dealing in lucrative ventures rather than looking over their shoulder in case a reporter was tailing them or prying into their personal affairs. Michael had done a lot of poking around.

How many of them were shadowing him anyway?

He reviewed the information he'd amassed on each of his key suspects. They were the ones most likely to seek revenge against him. He felt it in his gut. The feeling intensified when it hit him that Megan had played a vital role in his investigations by digging up evidence against them. What better reason to believe that one of these five suspects was behind her abduction?

But which one?

According to Willie, ex-con Gabe Rivard had secured his get-out-of-jail-free card and had the motive and opportunity to carry out his retaliation against Michael. He could have sent those francophone *vengeance* text messages to torment him about the potential grief awaiting him.

But although Rivard had openly announced his vendetta against him, it wasn't a given that he'd abducted Megan. Experience had taught Michael to give due consideration to what might not seem obvious at first. So although the ex-con was a credible contender, he had to keep his other four suspects in perspective too. They were behind bars, but that didn't mean they were powerless. He perused the information he'd collected on them again. Maybe something would jump out at him and point to Megan's abductor—and her location.

Trenton Barratt was the second suspect on Michael's list. The former businessman and philanthropist had donated substantial amounts to an elite college boarding school. Was he a kind and generous man? No way! He'd donated for fraudulent reasons.

Michael and Megan had been invited to that same private school for a career day presentation one winter weekend. On arrival, they learned about the suspicious deaths of two students. A treacherous ice storm blasted the area, closing down roads and cutting off power. They had no choice but to extend their stay. The school was located forty miles from the nearest town, and without access or communication to the outside world, it was impossible to get help.

The storm lasted a week, resulting in dwindling supplies of food and water, and no heat or electricity. Panic spread among staff and students with the discovery of more bodies and rumors of a killer in their midst. The dean lost control. It was absolute chaos!

When the dean requested Michael and Megan's help in investigating the deaths, they discovered a drug-manufacturing operation funded by none other than Trenton Barratt—with links to the Hells Angels.

Luck was on their side when they escaped death, and the storm cleared. The cops captured Barratt and his gang, but Megan and Michael's interactions with the businessman weren't over. They had to testify against him.

Faced with numerous charges, Barratt threatened them in court and vowed he'd go after them—no matter what. Michael didn't underestimate the convict's influential connections. Prison bars meant nothing to a man with far-reaching power.

Barratt was serving time in the same Quebec prison that had recently released Gabe Rivard. Michael shook his head. Talk about a coincidence. It wasn't much of a stretch to imagine that the two men had met, even spoken to each other. Barratt could have hired Rivard—or another member of the biker gang —to take him down. Or kidnap Megan.

Michael studied his notes on the third suspect.

He and Megan had visited their friends' lakeside resort one weekend in May. The trip promised to be a relaxing getaway— until a corpse showed up in a freezer!

Working alongside the police, Michael made a connection to a cold case he'd been investigating. Rusty Homer, a middle-aged man who had served decades in jail, had recently completed his term.

Rumor had it that the ex-con was tracking down partners who had abandoned him at the scene of a heist and driven off with millions in gold bullion. He was looking for revenge—and the gold bullion that hadn't been recovered. It was also rumored that his partners in crime had settled in the lakeside area. An increasing body count soon confirmed it.

Under normal circumstances, the ex-con would have been easy to locate. Problem was, he'd had reconstructive surgery. No one knew what the guy looked like anymore—not even the cops. Talk about a long shot! They might as well have been chasing a ghost. Before Michael and Megan realized it, Homer had lured them into a trap that almost ended their lives.

Shivers ran down Michael's spine. The guy was no ordinary adversary. He was a master of manipulation and an expert at playing mind games—especially with Megan. But they'd brought him down. They'd bruised his ego. They'd humiliated him.

Would Rusty Homer grab any opportunity for revenge?

He'd already proven that the extent of his retaliation was timeless. The way Megan had disappeared without a trace... It smacked of his cunning handiwork.

Michael had to remain vigilant. He didn't want to become the guy's next victim.

He filled a glass with water and took a few sips as he reflected on the fourth suspect. Another potential kidnapper.

On a business trip to Ottawa, Michael and Megan had entered their hotel room to find the corpse of a young woman on their bed. Nothing had rattled them more.

The victim's husband asked them to investigate. He was convinced his wife had been murdered and hadn't died from a drug overdose as the cops suspected.

Michael's investigation snaked along a winding road of legal innuendo and bureaucratic mumbo jumbo. He and Megan interviewed key witnesses endowed with a sense of entitlement —witnesses who hid wrongdoing behind deadpan expressions worthy of Oscar nominations.

One name emerged as they closed in: Randall Thorne. With Megan's knack for deciphering details, Michael gathered evidence that implicated the high-level bureaucrat in the young woman's murder. Thorne also faced additional fraud charges. Bonus!

After Michael and Megan testified against him in court, Thorne declared that he'd "even things out" with them one day. Michael didn't take his threat lightly—in the same way he hadn't taken the gun Thorne had pointed at his head lightly. Although no longer a notable official, the guy had connections to the right people in the right places. Without getting his hands dirty, his reach could extend well beyond his jail cell.

Thorne's ruthlessness gave Michael the creeps. The man remained a serious contender in Megan's kidnapping.

Michael reviewed the information on his last candidate.

Jane Barlow was the only woman on the list, but the cold-blooded killer didn't blink when it came to snuffing out a life. The former paralegal had devised murder plots and carried them out without a snag. That is, until she got caught.

To think that Michael had once dated her. He cringed.

It had been a brief fling. At first, he'd interpreted Jane's desire to be with him as a sincere interest, but she soon grew clingy. It was her obsession with him and his money that drove him to break off their relationship. She hadn't taken it well.

Then he met Megan. Bradford Publishing had recruited her to work with him on his crime novel that summer. Since they got together almost every day to discuss his manuscript, he got to know her better. Sure, he was attracted to her, but she was married. Michael respected that.

Things took a sudden downturn when Megan's husband

and a female companion were murdered. To top it off, the cops considered Megan and him as the main suspects. What a farce!

Michael asked his lawyer friend, Dan Cummings, to represent them. He was stunned when Dan hired paralegal Jane Barlow to assist with the case. Before he figured out what was happening, she'd manipulated the evidence and set Megan and him up as suspects in the double murders.

Their nightmare was far from over. With murder charges hanging over their heads, they fought to prove their innocence. Michael trusted that destiny had brought Megan and him together at the most opportune time and for a good reason. A normally cautious Megan defied the odds and saved his life in a final and violent confrontation with Jane.

Court testimony revealed that Jane was highly intelligent but suffered from a personality disorder and psychopathic tendencies. It explained her severe mood swings, bouts of intense rage, and lack of empathy. She'd learned to mimic emotions that were expected and had the ability to fool anyone. And she'd proven it.

The image of that last day in court moments before the guards took Jane away in shackles still haunted Michael. She'd stared at him and blown him a kiss while her eyes flashed, "You'll pay for this one day."

Was Jane a feasible suspect in Megan's kidnapping?

She'd been locked away for years in a multi-level woman's security prison in Quebec. Her opportunities for retaliation were as limited as the risk that she might escape.

Michael knew next to nothing about her family or friends, or whether she had other contacts on the outside. If by some miracle she did succeed in getting out, he'd be waiting for her.

He leaned back against the sofa, reflecting on the bigger picture. When it came to his job, his instincts had rarely steered him in the wrong direction. He'd learned to trust them.

Megan's unexplained disappearance, though, was another matter.

It wasn't as if the worst-case scenario had eluded him. Whenever he agonized over the possibility that Megan might already be dead, his whole world fell apart. How could he go on without her?

He gave his head a hard shake. He had to stop this negative thinking!

He reasoned that, if Megan were dead, those threatening messages would have stopped. They hadn't. What he needed to do was remain positive and keep moving forward with his investigation. He promised Connie that he'd find her daughter. He was determined to keep that promise—no matter the risk.

Determination was one thing, but Michael prided himself on being a realist too. He understood that the odds were stacked against him. To overcome them, he would definitely need Esposito's help. He didn't foresee a problem with that. The detective might even appreciate his input in ways he hadn't yet considered.

Michael gathered his papers. It was time to persuade Esposito and his investigative team that they couldn't possibly find Megan without his personal involvement.

15

—————

MICHAEL

Wednesday late afternoon

Michael sat across the desk from Esposito. He'd called the detective earlier to book an appointment with him. The purpose of his visit was twofold: He had inside information about recent Hells Angels' drug operations. He also had a list of convicts who'd met his criteria for the most likely suspects in Megan's disappearance.

In a face-to-face meeting with the detective, he could better explain the reasons behind his choice of perpetrators and persuade Esposito to involve him in the search for Megan. He needed to be part of their investigation. He wasn't going to take no for an answer.

He handed the detective a paper with the information Willie had supplied regarding a drug lab in Sainte-Adèle. "It's a new operation in the same area where the QPP busted the last one. Bad habits die hard."

Esposito glanced at it. "Good work. Our colleagues at the QPP will appreciate this." He set it aside without another word.

Michael questioned the detective's attitude. If he didn't know better, he'd say he seemed dismissive.

Next Michael handed Esposito his list of suspects. With murder as their common feat, the felons included a Hells Angels gang member, an illegal drug manufacturer, an armored car thief, a ruthless paralegal, and a corrupt bureaucrat. He could have sent the list by email, but he didn't believe it was safe to transmit such sensitive information over the web these days.

Besides, sending an email about heartless assassins made it all too real. Convicted murderers who wanted revenge on him was one thing, but targeting Megan? He couldn't accept that.

Michael elaborated on the reasons behind his choice of suspects. He cited his—and Megan's—personal experience with them, which at times had been life-threatening.

Esposito agreed that every suspect on the list was a feasible contender who could have played a part in Megan's kidnapping. While Michael had anticipated a more decisive response, Esposito placed the paperwork aside and sat back in his chair. "You've been busy."

Michael noticed his casual attitude again but said nothing. "Chasing the bad guys brings out the best in me. Where do we go from here?"

"*We?*"

"I can tell you more about each of these suspects than you'll ever find in court documents or prison records. Hours ago, an informant told me that Gabe Rivard had a contract out on me."

Esposito blinked. "He's one of your suspects. A local Hells Angels gang member, isn't he?"

"You got it," Michael said.

"Any idea of his whereabouts?"

"No. I was counting on your help to flush him out."

"We don't have the manpower to put a tail on him."

Michael translated it to mean he was on his own as far as

dodging bullets was concerned. "What about the other names on my list? The inmates?"

Esposito gestured toward it in an offhand manner. "I can request a status report from police headquarters on them."

Why was the detective reacting to his efforts with such triviality? Michael couldn't hold back. "What's the problem? Why are you treating Megan's case as if it isn't important?"

"It's not that." Esposito leaned forward, his expression somber. "Moments before you arrived, I received some news."

Michael's heart pumped wildly. "About Megan?"

The detective nodded. "I debated whether or not I should tell you. The information is incomplete, and I don't want to raise your hopes."

"Tell me, for God's sake!"

"The QPP notified us that they found her car."

Michael's throat constricted, and he could barely utter the words. "And Megan?"

"We don't know."

"What do you mean, you don't know?"

The detective went on. "The car was abandoned in a farmer's field outside Montreal. It had been set on fire. The QPP opened the trunk and found the body of a woman wrapped in a rug."

Michael gasped. It was as if someone had struck him in the stomach with a sledgehammer.

"We don't know the women's identity." Esposito's eyes reflected the compassion in his voice. "Forensics is performing the usual DNA and fingerprint analysis. I put a rush on it, but they won't have results before another twenty-four hours."

Michael said nothing. His mind had gone wild with a range of scenarios, one more macabre than the next.

Megan's mother. He'd promised her that he would dig up the truth, no matter how unpleasant it might turn out to be.

He needed to know.

But at the same time, he didn't want to.

"I'm not saying this to sound crude," Esposito said, "but if the victim is someone else, her identity might lead to Megan's whereabouts."

The chance that the victim might not be Megan gave Michael a glimmer of hope. "All the more reason I can help you with the investigation. I know how each of the suspects on my list operates."

The detective shook his head. "Sorry, the situation hasn't changed. I can't—and won't—involve you. I refuse to put you through that. However, the police will be asking for the public's assistance in providing clues. A missing person report about Megan will hit the news soon."

Michael placed his hands on the steering wheel. It was strange how he didn't remember leaving the police station and walking to his car parked a block away.

The discovery of Megan's abandoned car, though expected, had sent a jolt through him. That the perpetrator might have put her body in the trunk and set the car on fire was too much to fathom.

This can't be happening. He couldn't lose her. Not now. Not ever. They were planning to buy a home, build a future together...

Yet he had to prepare for the devastating possibility that he'd never see Megan again. His vision blurred and tears trickled down his cheeks.

No. He refused to accept she was gone. Besides, forensics had no conclusive results so far. The charred victim could be someone else. It *had* to be someone else.

Connie had asked if he'd told his parents about Megan's disappearance. So far, he hadn't.

What better time to call them than now?

He dug out his phone but wavered. He refused to get into another heated argument with his father and would tell him so.

Except that now, it was all about Megan. It was all too real. He had to tell his parents what happened. He tapped the familiar contact name on his phone.

His mother answered. Her soft voice was comforting, as were her words. He'd sought that solace whenever he needed to discuss important matters with her.

It was impossible to control the tremor in his voice or the raw nerves in his body while he told her about Megan. He held back from mentioning his suspect list and the gruesome evidence Esposito had shared with him earlier. It would have cast ugly shadows over what was already a terrifying event.

His mother's reaction was predictable. "Oh, how dreadful! That poor girl. Oh, Michael, you must be devastated. Any news from the police?"

"The cops are treating it as a missing person case," he said. "They have no tangible leads right now."

"Will you be helping them look for her?"

He didn't want to reveal that the cops had refused his assistance, so he improvised. "You can bet I'm going to do everything in my power to find her."

"I'm sure you will. Megan is a smart young woman. If she's in trouble, she'll try to find a way out. Stay confident that you'll see her again, Michael."

Her optimism gave him hope. "Thanks, Mom." He paused. "Is Dad there?"

"No, he went to a board meeting. He should be back soon. We'll be here if you want to call back later."

After they said they goodbyes, the tension in his body eased somewhat. His mother's supportive words had intensified his determination to stay strong and remain objective.

He set out to find Megan.

16

—————

MICHAEL

Wednesday late afternoon

Michael drove to *The Gazette* to meet with Derrick. Their earlier phone conversation had convinced Derrick that any of the five convicts Michael had singled out might be behind Megan's kidnapping. Accordingly, Derrick had given him the go-ahead to call the inmates from an office on the premises reserved for meetings with confidential sources.

"Keep the conversation simple, Michael," Derrick advised him after they'd entered the room equipped with a private phone line. "Handle it as if you're working on an investigative news piece. We can't risk getting on Detective Esposito's bad side by overrunning his territory."

"Don't worry," Michael said. "I'll play nice."

"Fill me in before you leave." Derrick left and closed the door behind him.

Michael drew the blinds in the glass-paneled room tucked around the corner from the open cluster of staff offices. He sat in one of two chairs at the table, then took a few extra seconds to relax before he made his calls.

He placed requests with the individual prisons to have four of the inmates on his list call him collect at *The Gazette*, namely, the illegal drug manufacturer, the armored car thief, the paralegal, and the bureaucrat. Since prisoners have rare contact with the outside world, Michael was counting on the curiosity that his name would generate. It wasn't as if they had anything better to do than kill time anyway.

He wasn't foolish enough to expect that all four convicts would call him back. If any of them held deep-seated grudges against him, they'd refuse to talk to him, let alone accept to cooperate with him.

While he waited for the phone to ring, he opened up his laptop. He clicked on an article about female prisoners he'd been researching in his spare time. He needed a way to get information from within prison walls before he could convince Derrick it was a worthwhile piece. His call to the Quebec prison where Jane Barlow was incarcerated might come in handy. If she returned his call, he'd use the opportunity to ask for her feedback about prison life from a woman's perspective.

He jumped when the phone rang.

Rusty Homer, the armored car thief and murderer jailed in a maximum-security prison in Ontario, identified himself, then asked, "To what do I owe the honor of your call, Michael?"

Michael flinched at the sound of his voice. His last interaction with the man had almost killed him and endangered Megan's life. He shut his eyes, forcing the memory away, and briefed him on her disappearance. "I'm trying to get a handle on the type of person who could have taken her."

"You mean you're trying to find out if I'm involved," the elderly prisoner said, chuckling.

There was no fooling this guy. "Are you?"

"I work alone. Besides, I have more important things to do with my time—like trying to get decent reading material. We have no access to the Internet or computers here. But you already knew that, didn't you?"

Michael was oddly reminded of a smug Hannibal Lecter and his fear of boredom. He could almost imagine a similar leer on his caller's face as the man skillfully implied his unspoken request. He took the hint and said, "I might be able to arrange something. How does a year's subscription to your favorite magazine sound?"

Homer cited a specific magazine, then said, "Make it two years and we have a deal."

Michael took his time to answer. Cops didn't make deals with prisoners in exchange for information. He contemplated whether or not he should give the felon's request further consideration, but time wasn't on his side.

Though he had no problem with sending Homer a two-year subscription, he didn't want to give this architect of mind games the impression he was a pushover. "Well..." he said, stalling. "Okay. Two years."

"I look forward to it." Anticipation ran through Homer's voice. "Now...about your problem. Did you receive a demand for ransom in exchange for Megan's safe return?"

"No."

A huff at the other end of the line. "Whoever abducted her doesn't want money. If it were about money, you'd have heard from the kidnapper by now. It's all about revenge for some perceived wrong."

Homer might as well have been speaking about a comparable stint that had landed him in jail. Regardless, the text messages Michael had received already indicated the sender was out for revenge. "Anything else?"

"Megan was more easily accessible than you. However, it doesn't mean you're no longer a target."

Nothing new. "Any insight on the kidnapper's *modus operandi*?" Michael hated himself for sounding so desperate.

"They play hide-and-seek games. They love to leave clues. You'll have to dig beneath the surface to find them."

For his next question, Michael especially welcomed the

insight of a man who'd been charged with kidnapping. "I have potential suspects. How can I gauge the feasibility of their respective involvement?"

"Ask yourself who would have the most to gain, then follow your gut. It's usually who you suspect the least."

The line went dead.

If Homer was right, Michael had to figure out which of his suspects had the most to gain. No easy task. For starters, each of them wanted Michael's head on a platter.

The next call came in an hour later from Trenton Barratt. The illegal drug manufacturer was in a maximum-security prison in Quebec—the same jail that had housed Gabe Rivard until recently. Because of their mutual links to the Hells Angels, Michael suspected that the two men might have a few things in common.

"I'm surprised to hear from you." Barratt coughed. "Are you calling to say you regret having testified against me? That you're sorry you destroyed my life?"

"No," Michael said. "I have no regrets."

"Then what do you want?"

Michael briefed him on Megan's disappearance. "Do you know anyone who might be out to get me?"

"Even if I did, why would I tell you? I don't owe you a damn thing." Barratt coughed again, a reminder that his health hadn't improved since the day Michael met him.

"Would you happen to know a former convict named Gabe Rivard? He was just released from the jail where you're serving time."

Barratt's gruff tone cut through the line. "Your question is irrelevant to me. How can you presume that I know everyone in this place?"

"I heard the guy has a vendetta against me."

"In that case, I'd like to shake his hand," Barratt scoffed. "If for some reason he doesn't get the job done, I'll come after you myself." He hung up.

Michael sat back in the chair and let out a slow breath.

Two callers down. Two more to go.

At six o'clock, a staff member from a Quebec prison phoned to say that inmate Jane Barlow wasn't available to return his call. When Michael asked why, the staff member merely repeated the message.

Although he hadn't been thrilled about reaching out to Jane, he was frustrated that he didn't get to speak with her. Maybe she'd made up the excuse to avoid talking to him. It wasn't as if she would have been eager to help him anyway.

A subsequent call from an Ontario jail confirmed that inmate Randall Thorne had refused to speak with him. No problem. It was normal for a confined bureaucrat to harbor hatred toward a crime reporter responsible for destroying his quasi government career.

Somewhat disheartened, Michael closed his laptop. He trudged down the hallway and passed the empty cubicles to Derrick's office. He tapped on his open door. "Got a minute?"

Derrick waved him in. "Any luck with your calls?"

Michael recapped his findings.

"That's fifty-fifty. Not too shabby. Any hunches?"

"The way I see it, Gabe Rivard is my best bet so far. The sadist." Every muscle in Michael's body tensed up. "The idea that some sleazy Hells Angels guy put his filthy hands on Megan and—"

"Stick to the facts. You'll drive yourself nuts imagining all sorts of things. It's been a long day. Why don't you go home and get some rest?"

Derrick was right. Michael didn't want to imagine *what ifs*. If he ventured down the rocky road, appalling images of what might be happening to Megan right now would drive him over the edge.

He had to stay focused.

And he had to stay away from the edge.

17

———

MEGAN

Wednesday late afternoon

Tiny's gravelly voice projected down the stairs like a blast from a BB gun. "Lardo! Get up here!"

Lardo turned off the TV with a click of the remote. "What do you want?" he growled back.

"I need help with the groceries."

"But you said I had to stay in the basement to watch her."

"Get your fat butt up here right now!"

Lardo pushed himself out of the chair and ambled across the basement floor in no apparent hurry. As he walked by, he looked at me and rolled his eyes. He thumped up the stairs, his feet landing hard on each step in a show of defiance.

It was my good fortune that he left the door open at the top of the stairs. Maybe they would inadvertently mention their boss by name or what they had in store for me. I strained to listen, hoping snippets of their conversation would filter down to me.

There was a rustling of bags and the sound of footsteps as

Lardo and Tiny carried the groceries back and forth across the foyer to the kitchen. After several trips, they began to chat.

"When are we leaving here?" Lardo asked.

"Soon I hope," Tiny said. "The old lady next door walks her dog up and down the street every day. I hate the way it barks at this house every time they go by."

"She rang the bell here two times. The dog barked real loud. We should leave here now."

"We can't leave."

"Why not?"

"We leave when the boss says so."

"But I don't like it here," Lardo whined. "I can't go outside. I can't do nothin'."

Tiny raised her voice. "Do you want to disobey the boss?"

Lardo said nothing.

"We have to store these cans in the bins by the garage door. Grab a bunch."

Bins? Was Tiny stocking food in bins to take with them? Would they be leaving here soon?

Silence fell between them as they carried on with their chores. I had precious little time to put the next step of my plan into motion.

My hands were shackled in front of me, so I was able to retrieve the metal shower hook from my pocket. I planned to leave my initials in as many places as possible so that Michael and the police would know that my kidnappers had held me captive here.

I lifted a corner of the rug under me and used the pointed end of the hook to scratch the letter *M* into the cement floor, then the letter *S*. I worked fast. Every second counted.

I inspected my handiwork. I could hardly see the letters. I'd have to press harder.

Voices upstairs. Lardo and Tiny were talking again.

"So when are we leaving?" Lardo asked.

"Are you dense? Why do you keep asking me the same

question?" Tiny shouted. "I already told you that we can't leave until we get the okay from the boss."

"But Tiny, we can't stay here. That woman and her dog—they'll bother us again."

"We have to follow orders. We can't disobey the boss. You know what would happen to us if we didn't do as we were told, don't you?"

"I know, Tiny. The boss will track us down and kill us."

"That's right. And it won't be fun."

"No, it won't be fun."

The boss will track us down and kill us.

I returned to the task at hand. I frantically repeated the strokes over the initials until the letters became more visible.

While I worked, I thought about Michael and my mother. They must have reached out and consoled each other. Michael would promise my mother that he'd find me, no matter what it took. In turn, she would ensure he was eating well so he could carry out his promise.

As the conversation dwindled between Lardo and Tiny upstairs, I worked faster, harder. I'd almost finished the letter *S* when Lardo's heavy footsteps sounded on the stairs.

I flipped the rug over to cover my initials. With no time to return the shower hook to my pocket, I hid it inside my fist.

"I have a special treat for you," Lardo said, his eyes shining.

I didn't know whether to rejoice or panic.

He grinned. "I found a yummy treat in the kitchen. Tiny hides goodies from me all the time. She thinks I'm dumb, but I fooled her. I looked in the pantry behind the boxes of cereal and found this." He held up a wrapped chocolate bar.

Chocolate! My mouth salivated. My body craved any type of nourishment. I'd eat the wrapper if I had to.

"We can share it." Lardo moved closer to me.

Fear gripped me. What if he noticed the shower hook in my hand? I had to prevent him from seeing it at all costs.

"No, thanks," I said. "I don't want any."

His expression scrunched up. "You sure?"

"Yes," I said, deeply regretting what I was giving up.

Lardo plodded over to his chair in front of the TV. He was settling in to watch hours of his favorite shows.

I silently exhaled. I didn't know how much longer we'd be here, but if I wanted to reinforce whatever bond we had going between us, I had to get him to talk to me.

As he grabbed the remote, I said, "Wait!"

Lardo grimaced. "Huh?"

"Can we talk instead?"

He put down the remote. "About what?"

"How did you get your name?"

"My mom gave it to me. She's gone now."

I didn't know whether he meant she was dead or had left town. I had to keep the conversation going. "I never heard the name of Lardo before."

"My real name is Leonardo."

"So why do people call you Lardo?" Tiny obviously did, but maybe someone else had initiated the custom.

He scratched his head. "The kids in school called me Lardo because I was bigger than them. It stuck. Everyone calls me Lardo now."

"Do you have any brothers or sisters?"

"A brother." He smiled. "His name is Nat. He's my younger brother. He's in a foster home. We don't see each other much. He calls me Lardo too."

As if on cue, Tiny shouted from upstairs, "Lardo! Come and get this tray."

While he obliged and went upstairs, I tucked the shower ring back in my pocket. A sudden spell of dizziness overcame me. I inhaled deeply and the room stopped spinning. I looked forward to dinner. Maybe I'd get a more generous portion this time.

Lardo arrived with our dinner tray. He handed me a bottle of water that barely contained any liquid and a slice of buttered bread on a plate. He sauntered away with his triple-decker sandwich of sliced meat, cheese, tomato, and lettuce, and settled in his habitual spot.

I swallowed the slice of bread within seconds. I'd starve to death soon—if I didn't die from dehydration before. Lack of fluids sped up the process. I could be dead within days. Why were they doing this to me?

Since Tiny had interrupted my conversation with Lardo, I tried to pick up where we'd left off. "Does your brother live near here?"

He put a finger to his lips and shot me a reproachful stare, then turned back to watch TV.

It dawned on me that I was only another vague obligation in Lardo's life—somewhere behind eating, watching TV, and following Tiny's orders. He had no interest in anything unless it stirred his appetite or caught his attention in the moment. What I'd considered a bonding and deepening trust between us was simply a deception I'd concocted out of desperation.

With my energy level dwindling from a lack of water and food, my eyes started to close by early evening. I fought to stay awake, but despite the boisterous TV programs Lardo watched into the late-night hours, exhaustion overtook my body.

The hardness of the cold, damp floor was my last thought as I drifted into a deep sleep.

18

JANE

Thursday morning

Jane Barlow always knew she could get away with murder. After all, wasn't it just a game? Pitting her sophisticated wit and strategies against the weak, pathetic efforts of her adversaries.

Destiny, however, prevented her from sharing her latest success with anyone. The last thing she wanted was to go back to jail.

The praise would come later when suspicions would begin to float and trigger nervous static in the air. *Who? How? Why?* The public, scratching their heads, would openly admire the brilliant circumstances in which the murder had been carried out without a hitch. And without a visible suspect.

The media coverage would hastily unfold, highlighting the conspiracies analyzed and the bewilderment emanating from the police press briefings.

She would record those moments of ultimate triumph to experience them over and over again.

Anger surged inside her, however, when she remembered

Michael and what they once had together. He couldn't expect to be part of her life after so cruelly rejecting her, leaving her to fend for herself. Yes, there was a steep price to pay for having neglected her.

Jane smiled. She wasn't as callous as most people thought. She would give Michael a chance to redeem himself soon. Very soon. She had to be patient. If she moved too fast, he might see through her ruse.

She'd spotted him from the upstairs bedroom window the other day, looking more handsome than she recalled. He knocked on the front door, but she'd already given Tiny and Lardo strict instructions not to answer. She watched as he walked away from the house and spoke with that irritating old woman next door.

Michael was perfect for her. As she was for him. Brains, money, and sex. Adrenaline pumped through her as the memory of those moonlit nights in bed with him surged to mind.

As much as she wanted to catch the surprise on his face when he linked her to Megan's disappearance, she had to stick to the plan. From her escape to Megan's kidnapping, it had been a risky—and thrilling—undertaking. No surprise there. Every aspect had played out as intended.

With one exception.

Tiny. The petite but gutsy woman had flirted with Michael at an all-night store and bragged about it afterward. "He's so cute," she'd told Jane, grinning like a fool.

Jane had barely contained her rage. Tiny's indiscretion could have ruined her entire plan. To teach the woman a lesson, she'd grabbed her and throttled her until she got bored with hearing her squeals.

Granted, Tiny wasn't a total write-off. Her relationship with Ken Reilly had proven useful. An attractive boyfriend with a penchant for get-rich-quick schemes, he came with a high price tag, but certain investments were worth it.

All the same, it was best to keep others in the dark about some things. Unknown to Ken, he'd guided Megan right into a trap. He had a convincing manner about him and, although the bouquet of flowers he offered Megan was a sappy gesture, it did the trick.

As for Tiny, as long as cash kept flowing in her direction, she would keep her drug supplier happy and her mouth shut. Speaking of her mouth... The burner phones that Tiny had used presented another problem. She'd sent text messages to Michael and Ken but hadn't ditched the phones afterward. Jane had to step in and remind her to do so. What a bother! As if she didn't have more important matters to take care of.

Then there was Lardo. The only thing he wanted was his next meal. Easy enough to handle. He'd be able to afford years of meals with the payoff she'd given him. If he lived that long. As soon as he served his purpose, she'd get rid of him.

Yes, diligence was imperative. Even if her plan was unfolding in a timely fashion, there was still the potential for something to go wrong. Not because of anything *she* did, of course, but because of the limitations of others.

Who was the weakest link in the chain? Tiny? Ken? Lardo?

It was Ken. He was the outsider. What would he do when he discovered how Tiny had cajoled him into an intricate kidnapping scheme? Would he betray her and expose her to the police?

Jane doubted it. That type—self-obsessed, self-preserving— would think twice about snitching to the police.

Two factors supported her conviction. First, Ken had readily accepted her generous cash payoff. Second, his relationship with Tiny, an ex-con and drug addict, whose identity would undoubtedly surface in connection with Megan's kidnapping, would raise questions about his integrity.

With that kind of evidence, would the police believe that Ken wasn't involved from the start? Even so, his loyalty was a factor. All the more reason to keep him within her scope.

Yes, she had everything under control. She wouldn't let anyone manipulate her anymore.

Not like her mother had. She had intimidated and lied to her, then ran off with another man when Jane was ten years old. She'd cheated her out of her childhood.

Her father hadn't been able to provide any better for her. Not in the manner she was entitled to, anyway. Having to wear second-hand clothes from thrift shops, go without makeup and so many things other teenage girls had access to...

Circumstances had driven her to shoplift. She grew adept at it too and avoided getting caught. When she turned eighteen, she did her father a favor and left home.

Jane blinked away the memories. She no longer had any reason to dwell on negative topics. Battling intrusive demons and hiding sinister secrets all her life had made her more resilient, more skilled at evading compromising situations. Guilt lay behind her. She'd acted according to plan and for the greater good. Hers above everyone else's.

She deserved a man who would fit into this cultivated life. A handsome, sexy man with a substantial bank account, to be precise. Michael fit the bill. Now that Megan was out of his life, Jane had to set him straight.

She twisted a strand of dark hair in her fingers. She'd spent the last five years behind bars. Away from Michael. Someone was going to pay for it.

Megan. It was all her fault. She'd messed with Michael's mind and forced him to be with her. If it hadn't been for her testimony in court...

It was payback time. She had contrived a slow and painful death for Megan. By the time Michael found her, Megan would be withered, unstable, and useless. He'd turn away from her and run to Jane, arms wide open, and they could finally be together.

She had to leave this old house soon. Michael mustn't find her. Not yet anyway. She had to put more distance between them before she contacted him. She could hardly wait to see him again, but she couldn't let impatience spoil her plan. Rushing into something this critical would ruin everything.

Megan. She was to blame. It was only fitting that Jane would use her as bait to lure Michael into her ploy. It would be like killing two birds with one stone.

Well, not exactly. Killing one bird and keeping the other in a gilded cage.

A smile crossed her lips, then vanished as she contemplated her next move.

Yes, someone had to suffer.

It might as well be Megan.

19

———

MEGAN

Thursday afternoon

Someone was coming downstairs. Light footsteps.

Not Lardo. He was sitting in a chair not far from me. Was it Tiny?

"Lardo? Are you there?" a young woman asked.

My skin crawled at the sound of a familiar voice that had once brought terror into my life. How was it possible?

Lardo bounded from his chair and tucked his shirt in his pants. Standing tall and erect, he gave the impression he was getting ready to salute someone.

Slender legs in high heels stepped onto the basement floor. A dark-haired woman in a jacket and matching skirt stood staring down at me. With all that makeup on her face, no one would have recognized her from her mug shot.

Jane Barlow!

Sentenced for my husband's murder and her attempts to kill Michael and me, she was supposed to be locked up in jail. How the hell did she get out?

Tremors spread through my body, and I fought to control

them. I refused to show her how terrified I was. I had to put on a brave front if I wanted to survive.

"Surprised to see me?" Jane crossed her arms and sneered at me. "Silly me. You can't answer with that tape over your mouth, now can you?" She leaned over and ripped it off.

I cried out in pain, convinced she'd ripped my skin off too.

"That's nothing compared to what I have in store for you." She smirked, as if she were the sole keeper of a plan too monstrous to share.

Tiny came downstairs with a tray of food and placed it before me.

Lardo moved up and removed my handcuffs.

"Eat up," Jane said to me. "We can't have you die before Michael finds you and sees you for what you really are—a sniveling bag of mush."

I warily observed the few ounces of water inside a plastic bottle, the two crackers topped with a bit of jam.

As if Jane had read my mind, she said, "Don't fuss. There's no poison in your food."

"Ironic words coming from you," I said, recalling how my husband had died at her hands.

"Now, now, Megan, we mustn't be rude to each other," Jane said. "After all, we're going to have to live together for a short while."

A short while? How long did she expect me to survive on these slim rations? Maybe she didn't.

As desperate as I was, I had to know. "How did you manage to get out of jail?"

She fixed her steely blue-gray eyes on me, eyes that were incapable of transmitting warmth or empathy. "It's immaterial. I'm here. That's all that matters."

Her gaze zoomed in on the diamond locket around my neck and she frowned.

Michael had given it to me years ago. It had belonged to his late grandmother, and I'd worn it every day since he'd declared his love for me. In earlier days, when Jane was dating Michael, she believed she was entitled to the locket—and a lot more.

Her mood shifted abruptly and she smiled. "I saw Michael the other day."

"That's a lie!" I said.

"He came right up to the front door. He even rang the bell, but we didn't answer. Right?" She looked at the others for confirmation.

Heads nodded in agreement.

"So close and yet so far." Jane kept her eyes on me, waiting for a reaction. "It's okay. We'll be together soon enough. Some of us longer than others, that is."

Her words froze the muscles at the back of my neck. I forced myself to meet her glare but she said nothing.

She turned to Lardo. "Make sure she eats. Don't forget to tape her mouth and cuff her afterward. Tiny, come with me."

Jane wanted to keep me alive. At least for a short while, she said. In what game had I become her chief pawn?

I awoke, confused. Darkness surrounded me. The floor was cold beneath me, and my back ached from the hardness of it. Where was I?

Doors opening and closing.

The clinking of bottles.

Muffled voices in the foyer upstairs.

I got my bearings. I was still in the basement of the house I'd visited. The one that was supposed to have a home showing. How long ago was that?

I tried to sit up, but my body refused to cooperate. My hands were freezing. My legs were numb. And I was so hungry.

The bulb in the basement ceiling lit up.

Lardo galloped down the stairs. "Get up! We're leaving!" He wore a light windbreaker over a new pair of jeans.

I watched as he unlocked the restraints around my hands and ankles, then slipped the handcuffs in his pocket. Assuming he'd forgotten, I pointed to the strips of tape over my mouth.

"No can do," Lardo said. "You might scream. Get up."

I could barely stand up. When I finally did, I felt light-headed and my legs buckled.

Lardo caught me before I hit the floor. "Whoa! Steady, girl."

He put an arm around my waist and helped me up the stairs. He kept his grasp on me even after we'd reached the foyer. We stood there, waiting. For what, I didn't know.

Jane and Tiny entered the foyer, their respective heels clicking on the ceramic tiles. Both women wore coats, which told me the weather had turned colder.

"Do you have the handcuffs?" Jane asked Lardo.

"Yes, boss." He handed them to her.

She pointed to the cardboard boxes and plastic bins piled by the door leading to the garage. "Put all those containers in the SUV."

"She's gonna fall if I let her go," Lardo said.

He was right. My legs felt like rubber.

"Go!" Jane said, spurring him into action.

Lardo made several trips to and from the garage. My guess was that the containers were filled with food supplies and other necessities that Tiny had purchased on her outings. After his final trip to the garage, he didn't return. He'd probably taken a seat in Jane's getaway vehicle.

"Did you do a final check of the house?" Jane asked Tiny.

"Yes," Tiny said. "I went into every room and made sure we left nothing behind. I switched on a couple of lights upstairs like you said."

"Fine. Now bring her to the bathroom." Jane gestured toward me. "I don't want any accidents in the car."

As soon as I entered the bathroom, I gingerly pulled off the tape covering my mouth. I was shocked to see that my skin was red and irritated. An ugly, itchy rash had formed.

I flushed the toilet, then bent over the sink and drank water from the tap. Who knew when I'd get another chance? On the other side of the door, Tiny would assume that I was washing my hands. I gently put the tape back over my mouth before I left the bathroom.

As we joined Jane in the foyer, Tiny said to her, "We're ready to go."

Jane ignored her. "Take off your jacket," she said to me.

Compared with their coats, my short-sleeved shirt wouldn't be enough to keep me warm. "No," I said.

Her eyes riveted into mine. "Take it off."

I was outnumbered, so I did.

Jane snatched my jacket, then handed Tiny a scarf. "Wrap this around her head and mouth. We don't want that nosy old bat next door to see her like this and call the police. Then put the handcuffs back on. Here."

Tiny wrapped the scarf as Jane had indicated and tied it tightly at the back of my head. She snapped the cuffs on my extended hands.

Jane folded my jacket and placed it over the cuffs. "Hold on to the jacket so it doesn't fall," she warned me.

There was no offer of a coat. At least I'd be in the car.

Jane held the door open while Tiny led the way into the garage. I stepped down onto the short staircase. My legs were unsteady, and I leaned against the handrail for support.

"Hurry up." Jane slapped me on the back.

Tiny grabbed my arm and pulled me down the steps. She broke my fall by pushing me hard against the hood of a black Honda SUV. I steadied myself.

Lardo stood next to the vehicle, gaping at Jane as if he were waiting for her permission to get in.

Jane closed the interior door behind her, then glared at them. "Why is that garage door wide open? Do you want the entire neighborhood to see what we're doing?" Her expression tightened in frustration.

Tiny and Lardo stared at her.

I glanced outside. It was dark and raining hard. I'd lost track of time, but a lit streetlamp was a sign it was night. The sound of raindrops hitting the ground was invigorating, as was the scent of grass and moist earth. I inhaled. As cold as it was, I appreciated breathing fresh air again.

"You're sitting in the back seat." Tiny nudged me forward.

As I moved toward the rear door, I noticed that my car wasn't parked where I'd left it on the street. It didn't surprise me, but what had they done with it?

My attention returned to the rain. I hadn't had a shower in days and had the sudden impulse to run out into the torrent.

Or just run!

My legs were shaky, and my head was on a sluggish merry-go-round, but I had to try. My life depended on it.

I sprinted for the driveway, my heart pounding.

"Get her!" Jane shouted.

I ran several yards before my legs folded under me. I hit the ground hard. The jacket over my bound hands broke my fall, but my knees suffered the consequences. Bloody scratches peeked through my torn pants, and pain shot through me like a thousand paper cuts.

Lardo's sturdy arms lifted me up. He kept a firm hold on me as he led me back.

"You fool!" Tiny dug a finger into my chest. "Get in!" She stepped back and opened the car door.

I had little chance of escaping from these horrid people, but I wouldn't give up. Not now. The end design was clear.

Jane slid in behind the wheel.

Lardo got into the back seat behind Jane.

As I was about to get into the car, a dog barked. The next-door neighbor's dog!

I turned and squinted into the downpour.

An elderly woman stood at the end of the driveway, holding an umbrella in one hand and a leash in the other. The dog continued to bark. The woman told Ginger to be quiet, but it pulled in our direction and barked even louder. It was all the woman could do to keep it from charging at us.

I had to act fast. I tugged at my jacket to expose my hands, and keeping them low so no one else would notice, I waved at the woman. Because of the downpour, I couldn't tell if she'd seen me or not.

I'd hesitated a second too long.

"Get in!" Tiny slapped the back of my head, prodding me to get into the back seat next to Lardo. She shut the door and got in beside Jane.

Lardo reached over to buckle me up. "Hey, we're leaving!" He snickered.

I could see Jane's eyes in the rearview mirror. Unemotional and calculating. Goosebumps rose along my arms as I contemplated what dire punishment she was planning for me.

As she backed out of the driveway, she commented on the woman and her dog. "That interfering neighbor won't be able to see us through the rain and these tinted windows."

"What about me?" Tiny asked. "She saw me up close when I answered the door and spoke to her."

"That's *your* problem," Jane said.

Tiny said nothing.

We drove down the street and around the corner. The pelting rain blurred my vision of homes and prevented me from seeing the names on street signs. The unlit homes told me it was later in the evening than I thought.

The clock in the dashboard confirmed my suspicions. It was eleven o'clock. Jane's strategy was at work. No one except the next-door neighbor had seen us leave. I clung to hope that the elderly woman would be able to identify us when the police finally came around.

When we stopped at a main intersection, Jane said, "Lardo, remove the scarf and the tape from her mouth. If she screams, it goes back on."

He slowly removed the items and put them aside, then surprised me when he reached for my jacket and placed it around my shoulders. Despite his kind intentions, I still felt cold to the core.

And hungry. Hungrier than I'd ever experienced before.

And sore. My body ached from having sat and slept on a cement floor. Without medication, the itchy rash on my lips and face would spread.

But the physical pain was nothing compared to the mental anguish of having Jane in control of my life. Although it filled me with dread, I'd soon find out what her plan was.

"Where are we going?" I asked her.

Jane eyed me in the rearview mirror and said, "Shut the hell up."

Lardo wagged a finger at me.

I retreated from him as far as my seat belt would allow. I silently vowed to accept whatever moments of freedom I could gain and not say another word that might worsen my situation.

Tiny rummaged through her handbag. "I need a smoke."

"No smoking," Jane said.

"Why not?"

"Because I said so."

I was leaning against the window and caught Tiny's grimace as she turned away from Jane. There was no love lost between those two either. Time would tell whether Tiny continued to play second fiddle to Jane's whims. Then again, the choice wasn't hers. Jane made those decisions. We were all dispensable in her view.

Although traffic was minimal, Jane drove within the speed limit. I wished she'd accelerate and get stopped by the police for speeding, but it wasn't meant to be. She was as cautious as she was calculating.

The heavy rain persisted, distorting my view of the city scenery. I glimpsed at the road ahead. My heart sank as Jane took an exit for the highway. I grappled with the reality that we were leaving Montreal behind. The chances of anyone finding me had now been considerably reduced.

Michael, my family, my friends. Would I ever see them again? I choked back the tears. If only I could tell them what was happening.

But I couldn't. My handbag was gone. It had contained my cell phone. Jane had no doubt given Tiny instructions to get rid of it right after I was abducted.

My head was pounding. I leaned it against the cool window. I hadn't eaten anything since... I couldn't remember when. I didn't even know what day it was.

The pitter-patter of raindrops was soothing. I must have dozed off because the next time I glimpsed at the clock in the dashboard, an hour had passed.

Lardo flipped open a laptop. Like his new jacket and jeans, was the laptop another gift from Jane?

The MSN news page popped up and a missing person report appeared on the screen. My photo was displayed with a caption that read: Montreal resident goes missing.

My pulse picked up speed. Yes!

Lardo quivered with excitement. "Hey! You're a reality star!" He laughed, smiled at me, then laughed again. "Hey, boss, she's in the news!"

"Shut it down!" Jane bellowed.

Lardo looked up. "Huh?"

"You heard me." Jane's eyes flashed at him in the rearview mirror. "Shut down your damn laptop!"

"Okay, boss." Lardo reluctantly obeyed.

Encouraged by the news report, I hid my joy and turned my head toward the window. The police were actively searching for me. I was certain that Michael had been the force behind their response to my disappearance.

Although the rain continued, the large green florescent signs along the highway were somewhat visible. They indicated we were heading north to the Laurentians.

No! The police couldn't possibly track us down in the vast wilderness of the area. Thousands of square miles of forest punctuated by hundreds of hotels, niche inns, cottages, and bed-and-breakfast resorts was a daunting challenge to anyone looking for us.

The further we rode from the city, the less chance the Montreal police had of finding me. Would they broaden their search to the rest of the province and ask for help from their colleagues in the QPP? Would they stop looking for me after so many days or weeks?

Not a chance. Michael would pressure the authorities to keep on going. He was relentless, if not courageous. He would take matters into his own hands to track me down if it came to that.

I had to remain confident that he would find me.

For now, I had to maintain a brave front in Jane's presence, even though I hated not knowing what cruel stunt she would bring to bear on me next.

20

———

MICHAEL

Thursday night

Michael's phone rang. It was Esposito.

"I received the security video from the homeowners on Parkhurst Street," the detective said. "I know it's late, but I had to handle an emergency earlier. Do you feel like dropping by the station?"

Michael's pulse accelerated. Finally—a promising lead. "You bet." He checked the time. Nine o'clock. "I'll be there by nine-fifteen."

He grabbed his jacket. He didn't bother to wait for the elevator but took the stairs four floors down to the main lobby. As he neared the entrance, he stopped. It was raining hard. In his haste, he hadn't bothered to grab an umbrella.

He was about to hold his jacket above his head and dash out to the parking lot when he spotted an elderly man and woman hastening up the path. He recognized Mr. and Mrs. Shank, a retired couple who lived on the floor below his.

Michael held one of the double doors open as Mrs. Shank

scurried in. He took a step back inside to give her heavyset husband more space to squeeze by.

A car came to a screeching halt in front of the building.

Shots exploded in the air!

Glass flew in all directions!

Everyone hit the ground!

Glass splinters embedded in Michael's arms oozed blood, but he ignored his injuries. He ran out and caught a glimpse of the car as it sped away from the condo. Tinted windows on a late-model sedan prevented him from seeing the driver and his accomplice—the shooter. The late hour and heavy rain foiled his efforts to catch any part of the plate number too.

It didn't matter. His instincts told him the shooter could only be one person: Gabe Rivard. The guy had probably spent the last days casing the condo, waiting for the right moment to take him down.

Michael ran back to the condo lobby, where Mrs. Shank was leaning over her husband. Her face had several superficial cuts but she was otherwise okay. Her husband lay on his back, moaning in pain, the right sleeve of his shirt drenched in blood.

"Please help him!" Mrs. Shank pleaded with Michael.

He pulled out his phone and called 911.

A balding man, who Michael recognized as the concierge, stepped out of the elevator and gaped in horror at the scene. He left but soon returned with a clean cloth to wrap around Mr. Shank's arm as a tourniquet and another for Michael's wounds.

Two police cars and an ambulance skidded to a halt in front of the building. While paramedics tended to Mr. Shank, officers briefly questioned Mrs. Shank, the concierge, and Michael.

Paramedics swiftly loaded Mr. Shank onto a gurney. The man assured his wife that he was fine and insisted she didn't have to come along.

"Nonsense," Mrs. Shank said, holding her husband's hand. "We've been together for forty years and we'll be together for many more." She rode off with him in the ambulance.

It had stopped raining. As the cops began to cordon off the entrance with police tape, Michael moved outdoors and reflected on the older couple's conversation. Their apparent devotion and consideration for each other made him think of Megan. How he missed her! Nothing hurt more than his heart right now.

Forensics arrived to collect crime scene evidence. Although the site had been contaminated by first responders and several residents, including himself, the team would work on a shooting scene reconstruction. The surveillance system camera in a corner of the lobby meant a video was also available for viewing.

Michael's thoughts returned to Mr. Shank. The unlucky tenant had taken a shot meant for him. What lowlife would try to take him down with innocent people around? Although he knew the answer, he was nevertheless astounded by the brazen attempt.

He'd almost forgotten about Esposito. He called him to explain why he hadn't shown up to view the Parkhurst security video. He was surprised when the detective said he received word of the shooting and would be there soon.

An unmarked police car drove up fifteen minutes later. Esposito got out and hurried up to him. He gave Michael's arms a once-over. "Flesh wounds. Lucky thing it was raining. Either that, or the shooter needs more practice. Any idea who the hit man was?"

"Your guess is as good as mine," Michael said, "but I'd put my money on Gabe Rivard. Any news on the other suspects on my list?"

Esposito nodded. "We received status updates on their behavior and activities. All have clean slates except for Randall Thorne. It seems he was trying to start a pyramid scheme in jail about a month ago. One of the prisoners got wise to him and taught him a lesson. He ended up in the infirmary with a broken jaw. He's still there."

Michael said nothing. It would explain why Thorne had refused to call him back at *The Gazette*. Either the guy didn't want to talk to him or couldn't. "A broken jaw? Something tells me he didn't fight back."

"White-collar criminals rarely resort to violence. All talk and no show."

"That wasn't the message I got when he was pointing a gun at me. Anyway, nothing prevents him from using his contacts on the outside. I bet he had lots of experience in delegating his dirty work to others."

"I'm not too certain about that," Esposito said. "I spoke with the investigator working the case. He confirmed that Thorne had operated within a limited scope. Which means he has no large-scale network to support efforts of retaliation on the outside."

Michael instantly eliminated Thorne from his suspect list. "What about the other three names on my list?"

"What about them?"

"Didn't investigators review their case files too?"

Esposito did a double take. "Do you realize what you're asking? I'd need extra resources and a lot more time to get that sort of investigation underway."

Undaunted, Michael tried another approach. "Has anyone in your department called those suspects directly?"

"It's pointless. They don't talk to cops. They don't talk to reporters either."

Michael had evidence to the contrary, but he didn't want to reveal the ace up his sleeve. Besides, it sounded as if Esposito was trying to discourage his involvement again. "Which leaves us with Gabe Rivard, except..."

"Except what?"

"The clues don't add up. If Megan was going to a home showing, she would be wary if someone like Rivard approached her there."

The detective shrugged. "Maybe he shadowed her after she left. He could have caught up to her later."

"Sounds more like his style."

"We'll increase our efforts to find him." Esposito motioned toward the surveillance camera. "We'll get a copy of the system video here too."

"The concierge is over there if you want to ask him." Michael gave a nod toward the balding man who was speaking with other residents near the elevator.

While Esposito spoke with the concierge, Michael looked out at the street. Vehicles from local TV stations were pulling up and getting ready to film the premises. Damn! He needed to ask the detective one last question before he dashed upstairs to avoid questions from the TV crew.

He was about to enter the foyer when Esposito exited, phone in hand. "I'll be there in ten minutes." He tucked his phone away. "I have to go," he said to Michael, edging toward the path. "Take care of that arm."

"Wait. What about the Parkhurst Street video?"

"I don't know when I'll make it back to the station. It won't change anything if you come by tomorrow morning to view it." He left, pausing only to give the media a brief statement before he drove away.

Michael used tweezers to pull out the shards of glass from his arms, then applied antibiotic ointment to the wounds. After he'd wrapped his arms with bandages from a first-aid kit, he moved to the kitchen to satisfy a need for inner comfort.

Retrieving a bottle of red wine from the pantry, he filled a glass. He needed to wind down from the day's events. Most of all, he needed to sleep, but sleep didn't come easily to a restless mind.

He sat in the living room and dug out his phone. He wanted to reach one more person before he would call it a night.

Willie didn't sound surprised to hear from him. He was used to getting calls from Michael at all hours. "Felons like Gabe Rivard know how to disappear," he said in response to Michael's question about the ex-con's whereabouts. "They know all the tricks."

"The license plate might be visible on the surveillance video from the condo," Michael said. "Even with a partial, the cops might be able to track down the car."

"You can be sure he was driving a stolen car. The cops will never find it."

"Why not?"

"All Rivard had to do was drive it into an auto body shop run by the Hells Angels. They have crews that can dismantle a car in no time. Trust me, they are already selling the parts."

"So it's a dead end."

"For the car." Willie chuckled lightly. "It is not the end of your vendetta, though. After things cool down, Rivard will try again when you least expect it. Stay safe, my friend."

Although Gabe Rivard was short and wiry, he had a reputation for surprise attacks. Michael hated having to check around every corner and along every street, waiting for the ex-con to pop up. There had to be a way to draw him out...

He sat back on the couch and clicked the remote to catch the late-night news. The cops must have issued a statement about Megan by now.

He jerked up when a local report ran a brief clip about the shooting incident at the condo. It showed him standing outside, but the distance from the street and the tall trees would prevent anyone from recognizing him or identifying the building.

Lucky break. He exhaled with relief. He wouldn't want to worry his parents or Megan's mother even more.

The next clip showed Esposito announcing to reporters outside that a resident had suffered gunshot wounds but would survive. He made no mention of the suspected shooter or motive before he rushed off.

Michael's pulse picked up speed when the broadcaster announced that a Montreal woman named Megan Scott had been reported missing. A police spokesperson stated they had tangible leads on a potential perpetrator in what they alleged was a kidnapping incident.

As Megan's photo and a brief description lingered on the screen, Michael choked up. She was his life partner, and he would never forgive himself if something happened to her. He half-listened as the spokesperson encouraged the public to come forward with any information that could help the police in their search for Megan.

Michael turned off the TV and closed his eyes. He had to stay strong. He had to concentrate his efforts on finding Megan if it was the last thing he'd do.

Connie. She'd probably seen the missing person report about Megan on TV. The news would increase her optimism that the cops were finally doing something. He was about to call her, then stopped. It was late. She might be asleep.

His parents were night owls, though, so there was a chance they were still up.

He picked up the phone. It rang before he could make the call.

"Hello, Michael," his father's deep voice came across the line. "We saw the news report about Megan on TV."

"I saw it too," he said.

"Your mother told me you've been working with the police."

"Yes, I'm helping them in any way I can."

A long pause, then his father's voice boomed, sounding like the typical Darren Elliott interrogating his company directors at a board meeting. "Why is it taking so dam long? What are the tangible leads the police claimed they have?"

Michael stiffened. "I'm not at liberty to discuss that."

"If this situation in any way involves a ransom demand—"

"There was no ransom demand."

His father huffed in annoyance. "They should have offered a reward for information from the start. Money makes people talk."

Money isn't always the answer, Michael held back from saying. "I'm on top of it, Dad."

"I certainly hope so. Your mother wants a word. Susan, here's Michael." There was a crackling noise as his father passed the phone.

"Michael, I'm so sorry you're going through such a horrible ordeal," his mother said softly. "Would you like us to come over and stay with you?"

"No, Mom. I'm not home most of the time. I'm working."

"I understand." She lowered her voice. "Don't pay any attention to your father. He means well, but he has a hard time expressing it. Believe me, he's as distraught about Megan as I am."

"He could have fooled me."

"I know you and your father have had your differences over the years, but this is a situation that calls for family unity. We have to support one another, not squabble."

She was right. This wasn't the time for family disputes. "Sorry, Mom." He checked the time. "It's late. I'll call you once I get more news about Megan."

They said their goodbyes.

Michael rested his head against the back of the sofa and reflected on the recent TV coverage about Megan. With this latest news release, the cops had provoked the kidnapper into feeling pressured. Their statement about having "tangible leads" would make any criminal doubt himself and review his steps in case he'd screwed up. It was a strategic move on their part.

Now it was time to put his own strategy into action.

21

MEGAN

Thursday night

According to the clock on the dashboard, an hour and a half had gone by since we'd left Montreal. The road signs along the way indicated that we were in lakeside country.

The pelting rain had stopped, but the narrow road was wet and slick. Guided by sporadic florescent posts on the shoulder of the road, Jane drove at a reduced speed. The high beams from the occasional vehicle in the oncoming lane lit up the unwavering determination in her eyes as she concentrated on reaching her destination.

"I'm glad you're driving," Tiny said to Jane. "It's so dark, I can't see a thing."

"I grew up not far from here," Jane said. "You have to know your way around and keep alert, especially at night. It's easy to hit wildlife."

"Wildlife?" Tiny echoed.

"Deer, rabbits. Especially bears." She turned on the radio. A pop tune was playing on a local station. She raised the volume and lightly tapped the steering wheel in time with the rhythm.

Tiny took the hint and cut short their conversation.

A news report interrupted the music moments later. The police were expanding their search for me to municipalities outside Montreal.

Fantastic news! I hid a smile.

Jane swore and turned off the radio. In an abrupt show of anger, she pressed down on the gas. The SUV surged forward.

"Hey, slow down!" Tiny shouted.

Jane swung her arm and hit Tiny hard in the face. "Don't tell me what to do! And don't yell at me! Ever!"

Tiny moaned in pain. "You gave me a nosebleed." She reached into her handbag for facial tissues.

"You got off easy. If I wanted to, I could have—"

A loud bang sounded. The vehicle wobbled, then swerved to the left into the oncoming lane.

Tiny screamed.

Jane clutched the steering wheel and maneuvered the SUV until it straightened out. She guided it onto the shoulder and came to a stop. "It's a blowout. Lardo, go take a look."

Lardo got out and circled the SUV to inspect the tires. He soon returned. "You were right, boss. It's a blowout. There's a piece of metal in the rear tire on the left."

Jane turned on the hazard lights, applied the parking brake, and popped open the tailgate. "Change it. You'll find a flashlight and the tools you need back there."

"But—but boss, I never changed a tire before."

Jane turned to Tiny. "Go help him."

"It's not my—" Tiny began.

Jane glared at her.

As Tiny opened the passenger door, the overhead light went on, and I caught a glimpse of her. She'd inserted tissues up her nose to stop the bleeding.

Equipped with the spare tire and tools, the duo hunkered down to work on their task. Jane opened her window to overhear their conversation.

Soon Lardo and Tiny started arguing about how best to proceed.

Jane swore and climbed out of the SUV. Over the next fifteen minutes, she leaned over them, giving out orders and hollering at them to hurry up. Her impatience caused them to fumble the task all the more.

Her urgency was understandable. She wanted to avoid the chance that a police officer might stop by, check inside the car, and notice that I was bruised and handcuffed.

Not to mention her apprehension that the officer might recognize me as the missing woman from Montreal—or her as an escaped convict.

The possibilities would have been humorous if current circumstances weren't so terrifying.

I held my breath as a pick-up truck in the opposite lane slowed down, its headlights reflecting off the wet road.

A driver wearing a cowboy hat got out and took a few steps toward the SUV, then stopped. "Need any help?" he asked, the brim of his hat casting a shadow over his face.

I was about to scream but stopped. I didn't want to endanger the driver's life. Lardo might kill him at the snap of Jane's finger.

Jane had her back to me and was talking to the driver. Lardo and Tiny were crouched by the tire. I reached for the handle, knowing that opening the car door ever so slightly would activate the overhead light. With a slow and steady force, I pried it open. I swiftly raised my shackled hands and waved them at the truck driver.

"Like I said, thanks anyway," Jane was saying to the man. "We're almost done here."

"Okay." The driver gave her a nod and drove away.

My heart sank.

The man's cowboy hat had prevented me from seeing his face, so I couldn't tell if he had noticed me. There was nothing I could do about it now.

And yet, I had to do something.

My pulse rate soared as an idea formed. It was risky, but it was my last chance to escape.

I pushed open the door and darted into the opposite lane, hoping that another car was heading this way.

"Lardo, go get her!" Jane yelled.

I heard the thumping of feet behind me.

A large hand reached around my waist and lifted me in the air.

"I got her!" Lardo carried me back to the car. He laughed and snorted as if he'd won a prize. He set me down but kept a firm grasp on me while he opened the door to the back seat.

Jane's expression hardened in anger. "You'll regret this," she said to me. "Get in." She asked Lardo, "Are we ready to go?"

"Yes," he said. "Ready, boss."

"Put everything back in the SUV, except for the flashlight. We'll need it later."

Once everyone was seated and buckled up, Jane steered the vehicle back onto the road. I avoided looking at her in the rearview mirror. I'd already been subjected to enough of her evil eye, or *Il Malocchio*, as my mother and her Italian relatives said about people who were envious and wished you bad luck.

Jane soon announced, "It's not much further now."

Was our destination a cheap motel or a cabin in a rural town? I couldn't imagine Jane putting us up in some fancy hotel —especially if she was determined to keep us all invisible.

Jane veered left and drove down a stony path through a thick forest. She slowed down and took a right at a fork in the road, then another left. She came to a stop and turned off the engine. "We're here."

I stared out the window. A glistening reflection indicated a lake in the distance. On my right was the faint outline of a two-story log cabin bordered by trees and low shrubbery.

Who would ever find me here?

We stepped out of the vehicle, Lardo keeping a firm hold on

my arm. Which was fine by me. I had no intention of running off into the black of night.

"Lardo, you can come back for the supplies later," Jane said. She clicked the key fob to lock the SUV.

She lit the way with the flashlight, and we climbed a short flight of wood stairs. The screen door and exterior door were unlocked, which surprised me. Did she own this property? Did she know someone who did? She entered the cabin and turned on the lights.

We followed Jane through a rustic kitchen that held an old-fashioned wood table and chairs for six. Beyond, a central space opened up to a sitting area on the left. Two bulky sofas gave the impression they'd been salvaged from a different era. A wood-burning fireplace hugged a corner. To the right, a staircase led upstairs to the bedrooms.

I felt dizzy and almost fainted, but Lardo grabbed me and steadied me. "Where do you want her, boss?"

Jane snatched my jacket. "You won't be needing this." She pointed to a door located to the right of the staircase. "In there."

Lardo hauled me across the floor and opened the door to a three-foot-square closet. He hesitated. "In here, boss?"

"Yes." Jane smirked at me.

I was horrified. "No! Please, don't do this! I can't stand small spaces!" I tried to break away from Lardo, but I was handcuffed and at a disadvantage in every aspect.

"The best part about having a cabin in the woods is that you can scream as loud as you want, and no one would hear you." Jane laughed, then stopped abruptly. "Lardo, wait!" The hatred in her eyes seared through me as she came up to me. "It won't be long now. You'll be dead soon, and Michael will take his rightful place beside me. Get her out of my sight."

Lardo shoved me inside the closet and swiftly closed the door.

Darkness enveloped me.

I panicked.

"No!" I sprung forward and passed my bound hands along the surface of the door—or what I assumed was the door. But the surface was smooth and there weren't any partitions or a doorknob. Even though I couldn't see a thing, I was positive I'd headed straight for the door.

I moved to the right and repeated my search. I made my way around the closet, exploring every inch of the surface, but the result was the same. Having lost my bearings, I pounded my fists against the wall. "Let me out!"

Lights suddenly flooded the closet. Flashing strobe lights.

I instantly shut my eyes. Unexpected bright light—even a sunny day—often triggered migraines and pain so debilitating that I couldn't move or even think. My breathing quickened as I awaited the nausea that usually accompanied these attacks.

Loud, screeching music blasted through the air and I jumped. I traced the source to a speaker in the ceiling, then shut my eyes again. Tiny and Lardo would surely complain about the noise and put an end to this madness.

But nothing happened to stop the strobe lights or the deafening, hammering music. How long would this go on?

I squinted. Seamless white walls all around me. Were they insulation panels? Sound-blocking panels? If so, it meant my kidnappers weren't exposed to the same noise level on the other side of the door.

I noticed a hairline crack in one wall. The door! It had no handle but that didn't stop me. I sat on the floor, flung my shoes off, and kicked at it with all the strength I could muster. "Let me out of here!"

But no one answered my plea.

Exhausted, I stopped.

The soles of my feet hurt from battering them against a hard surface. Who was I kidding? The entire closet had been custom built and probably lined with an industrial material like sheet metal. As far as I could tell, there was no space for air to enter.

No air. Is this what Jane had planned for me? Was I going to suffocate to death?

Anxiety mounted inside me. I scanned the ceiling and spotted a minuscule vent. Air was circulating in here after all.

But those horrible flashing lights! They were unbearable. I squeezed my eyes shut.

Worse than the physical pain was the plausible explanation behind the strobe lights and earsplitting, thrashing music, and it terrified me.

Torture. Jane intended to use these classic techniques against me in the worst way.

I kept my eyes shut and huddled in a corner. I placed my manacled hands over my eyelids. The handcuffs prevented me from reaching my ears, increasing the chance that I could lose my hearing if the loud music continued.

My heart was beating so fast, I was certain it would burst out of my chest. Nausea mounted inside me, and I swallowed hard. Could I withstand this torment much longer?

The noise and lights stopped. Thank goodness! I waited for someone to open the door and let me out, but no one did.

Five, maybe ten minutes went by. It was so hard to judge the time.

The strobe lights and loud music started again.

No! Please stop!

I crouched in a corner, my face to the floor, and tried to block it all out. I refused to let Jane win. She wasn't going to drive me crazy.

She'd almost succeeded in pushing me over the edge years earlier. She'd lied and tricked everyone into believing Michael and I were responsible for my husband's death.

She was a master illusionist. A convincing one at that. A twisted, brutal, conniving woman who thrived on inflicting pain on others to get what she wanted. Despite her training in the judicial system, she lost her moral compass—if she'd even had one to begin with.

Jane was attacking me with a vengeance I hadn't foreseen. She was trying to drive me insane with loud, thumping music and bright, flashing lights, but she wouldn't win.

My mind was strong. I forced myself to focus on something else. Pleasant thoughts. Yes.

I imagined the new two-story house Michael and I would eventually buy. We'd fill it with modern furniture and add touches of retro and antique. I envisioned a large island in the kitchen where I'd prepare our meals and yummy desserts.

The lights and music stopped.

Darkness and silence surrounded me again.

The ringing in my ears worried me. Was it a sign of hearing loss? Would the damage be permanent?

The strobe lights and piercing music started up again.

Then they stopped.

Then they started again.

I lost track of time. Of everything rational.

I'd fallen into a void.

22

———

MICHAEL

Friday morning

Something vibrated against his shoulder. Michael awakened to discover his cell phone on the bed next to him. How he'd managed to fall asleep on top of the bedcovers was a distant memory—one best left to dissipate in the fogginess of the moment.

He picked up his phone. He didn't remember setting it to silent last night, but the ringtone was definitely off.

Dan, his lawyer friend in Toronto, had left him three voice messages this morning. The last one, seconds ago. He could have heard about Megan's kidnapping by now and called to express his concern. He'd follow up with him later.

Megan.

The nightmare of the last week rushed back. He couldn't imagine a life without her. She was the reason he looked forward to each new day. From her cheery smile on waking up every morning, to her goodnight kiss before they fell asleep, he'd come to anticipate those spirited signs of her affection. It meant the world to him. *She* meant the world to him.

They'd created memories together. Some good. Others not so good—like the times she'd accompanied him on investigative ventures that had unexpectedly turned dangerous. They'd flirted with death and survived. She'd saved his life on more than one occasion when he dared to go a step too far.

And now she might be fighting for her own life.

No. He didn't want to go there. Without Megan by his side, he'd be a shadow of himself. Nothing would have the same meaning. Not his career. Not his hopes. Not his dreams.

He stretched and pain shot through his arms, bringing back the gruesome scenes from last night's brazen attack. His prime suspect was still Gabe Rivard. The ex-con had fired a gun at him, injuring innocent victims.

Criminals shooting at one another in city cores, busy malls, public parking lots... Senseless killings had become the new norm these days. It was plain crazy.

He took a shower to shake the sleep from his body, then applied clean bandages to his wounds. He got dressed and headed for the kitchen, where he brewed a pot of Colombian coffee. Megan's favorite.

He filled a cup and sat at the table while he called Dan. As he suspected, his friend had caught yesterday's late news report about Megan.

"I can only imagine how distressed you must be," Dan said. "Why didn't you call me?"

"I left you a message."

"I'm so sorry, Michael. I've been in court the last while. Tell me exactly what happened."

He recapped the events leading to Megan's disappearance and how she hadn't returned his calls. "She was kidnapped. There's no other explanation."

There was a flutter of noise at the other end of the line. Dan was probably reaching for a hankie to pat perspiration from his brow—a condition that flared up whenever he grew tense.

"I'm absolutely stunned," Dan said. "I can't believe someone would want to hurt Megan."

Michael's lip quivered. He couldn't speak. How could he go on without her?

"How are you holding up, buddy?"

He fought for composure. "I feel as if my whole world is about to come crashing down on me. I never realized how afraid I was of losing her until now." His throat tightened up and he swallowed. "But I have to go on. For Megan's sake."

"Do you have any likely suspects under consideration?"

He would have considered Dan's question intrusive had he not worked with him on a handful of criminal cases over the years. He'd learned more about the court system processes from their investigative stints together in Toronto than any books had ever taught him.

"Gabe Rivard is my key suspect. He's an ex-con with a publicly proclaimed vendetta against me. He also happens to be a member of the Hells Angels that I helped put behind bars for drug trafficking. I told the cops he might have kidnapped Megan as an act of revenge."

"You said he was an ex-con," Dan said.

"Right. He was released from jail this week, so the timing fits."

"He's your sole suspect?"

"I have others, but he's at the top of my list."

"Any particular reason?"

"You bet. He took drive-by shots at me in front of my condo building yesterday."

"For Pete's sake! Are you okay, Michael?"

"I have superficial wounds. No big deal. Another tenant in my condo was hit, though. An ambulance took him to the hospital. He'll be fine."

"So you suspect Rivard abducted Megan to get back at you?" A hint of skepticism filtered through Dan's voice.

"It's all about revenge. He targeted Megan, but..." Another thought diverted Michael's focus.

"But?" Dan echoed.

"Someone else might be involved too." Michael recounted Esposito's disclosure about a mystery man meeting Megan in front of a Parkhurst Street home. "The detective asked me to view a security video they obtained from that home. I'll be dropping by the station this morning to view it."

"It's feasible that more than one person could have been implicated in Megan's disappearance. These things take time to plan."

"That's why I'm keeping my options open. Rivard might not turn out to be the only suspect. Like you said, it takes time to set up a complex kidnapping scheme. Aside from the driver in the getaway car, Rivard could have had extra help. The mystery man in the video might be it."

Dan heaved a sigh. "I hate to add to your problems at a time like this."

"What's up?"

"I have more bad news."

"It can't get any worse than this. Go for it."

"Jane Barlow escaped from jail."

Michael's blood turned cold. It took him a long second to grasp the significance of Dan's revelation. "How did she manage to escape from Joliette Institution? It's a multi-level security prison."

"Actually, she was in a hospital."

It explained why Michael couldn't reach her in jail. "A hospital? Was she sick?"

"No. She was scheduled for medical treatment of a cut she'd sustained in a fight with another prisoner. She needed stitches."

Michael ran a hand through his hair. "Wasn't she escorted? Supervised?"

"Prisoners usually are," Dan said.

"When did this happen?"

"Wednesday."

"Damn!" Michael pounded the kitchen table, spilling his coffee. It had become a habit lately. He ripped a paper towel from the roll to mop it up. "Security didn't do their job. They should have known what she was capable of. They should have sent an army of guards to escort that snake in the grass to the hospital."

"I couldn't have said it better myself."

"How did she evade the guards?"

"By exercising her usual *modus operandi*," Dan said, irony filtering through. "She struck the nurse with something and rendered her unconscious. Then she strolled out—right past the guards."

"How? Wasn't she wearing a prison uniform and handcuffs when they brought her there?"

"They had to remove her handcuffs for the treatment. After she knocked out the nurse, she removed her prison uniform and put on the nurse's white coat, surgical mask and cap, and eyeglasses. A foolproof getup. Like I said, her typical MO."

"No kidding," Michael said. "Jane never left anything to chance. You can bet she had an accomplice waiting outside in a getaway car."

"The police will definitely review the hospital surveillance video for leads." Dan hesitated. "You do know that the hospital is about an hour's drive northeast of Montreal, don't you?"

"I do." Michael weighed the likelihood that Jane had chosen Montreal as her destination. Was she so reckless as to return to a city where her photo had appeared in media headlines for months on end and risk being recognized? Where a court had eventually found her guilty of a double murder?

Or would she settle in an obscure Quebec town where nobody knew her and take on a different persona? She was an expert at that.

"She won't get far," Michael added, more to allay his fears

than anything else. "It's odd that I didn't hear anything about it on the news."

"The police delayed issuing a country-wide alert to the media. There was some confusion and misinformation at the prison regarding Jane's actual whereabouts."

"How did you find out?"

"A contact in prison administration just called me," Dan said. "He knew I'd counseled you and Megan in preparation for Jane's murder trial years back."

He appreciated Dan's discretion in not regurgitating Jane's role in the events involving the double murders. That horrific episode had stirred up a volatile period in Michael's life—one that he'd almost succeeded in obliterating from his memory, only to have it rise from the ashes now like a defiant phoenix.

"Michael?"

"Sorry. I was thinking about how long it had taken Megan and me to get over Jane's intrusion in our lives...how she almost destroyed us. Now she's on the loose again. I'm having a hard time wrapping my head around it. Who knows what goes on in that warped mind of hers?" Anger stirred inside him and he cursed her under his breath.

"I know where you're coming from," Dan said. "What a waste of talent! She was a brilliant addition to my Toronto staff as a paralegal. It's unfortunate that her Borderline Personality Disorder made her so unpredictable."

Michael hadn't told Dan about his brief intimate relationship with Jane. The two men were working on a court case in Toronto at the time. Since Jane was on the opposing legal team, his relationship with her would have been a conflict of interest. For that and other reasons, Michael broke up with her instead.

He expanded on Dan's claim. "Jane's BPD wasn't an excuse for murder. Her psychopathic behavior was."

"That's a given," Dan said. "No one was surprised—least of all me—when she was sentenced to twenty-five years in jail.

The hardest part was having to explain to my colleagues in the legal world why I'd hired her."

An ominous possibility crossed Michael's mind. "What if Jane had a hand in Megan's kidnapping? She had lots of time to launch her plan before she made her escape."

"She would have needed outside help."

"It's a long shot, but maybe she got a hold of Gabe Rivard and worked something out that was mutually beneficial."

"Anything's possible."

"Dan, I have to believe that Megan is still alive. It's the only thing that keeps me grounded. No matter what, I'm going to find her."

"I don't doubt you will." A shuffling of papers. "Michael, I hate to run out on you at a moment like this, but I have a court date. If there's anything I can do to help, please let me know. And keep me posted."

"You bet."

Michael slipped into his jacket minutes later and drove to the station to meet Esposito. The detective had told him that viewing the Parkhurst Street video wouldn't change anything. He didn't know what he meant by that. Maybe Esposito had decided that the video offered no viable leads.

Michael hoped he was wrong.

23

MICHAEL

Friday morning

Seconds after Michael sat down to view the security video from the Parkhurst Street home, he recognized the dark-haired man in a black jacket and khakis.

"That's Ken Reilly," he said. "He's a real estate agent at MRG."

"That's right," Esposito said from across his desk. "How do you know him?"

"I saw him at MRG," Michael said. "Brett Paquette, my agent, works there. How did you find out it was Ken?"

"From the video." The detective showed him an enlarged printout of a video frame. "With a description of Ken's car and a partial of his license plate, we were able to track him to MRG. I interviewed him there earlier today."

"Did you arrest him?"

"No."

"Why not?"

"Because he claims he was set up."

"How?"

Esposito hesitated. "The allegations I'm about to share with you remain within these walls. Understood?"

"No problem," Michael said.

"Ken Reilly told us he was hired to handle the private sale of a home. The seller was a young woman he'd met years ago. She told him her aunt, the owner of the house, had recently passed away. She gave him five thousand dollars in cash to bring Megan to the home showing, claiming she was an old friend. She promised him extra if he closed the sale."

"Where's the house?"

Esposito's brow creased. "Michael, you know I can't disclose that information. I can confirm, however, that it appears to have been vacated."

"What about the woman's niece? Were you able to track her down?"

"The name Ken gave us didn't check out. We tried to contact the actual property owner by phone. There was no answer. No answer when we knocked on the front door either. We spoke with neighbors and called local hospitals and funeral homes. We've got nothing so far."

Michael's instincts bumped up a notch. "I bet Ken is hiding something."

"He insists he was duped. He's extremely distressed about what happened to Megan."

Michael raised his hands in disbelief. "And you're buying that crap from him?"

"It's all on him if's he's lying," Esposito said. "He knows we can charge him with kidnapping if we find evidence that directly implicates him."

"Perps lie through their teeth. My gut tells me he's holding back on revealing other stuff too."

"Maybe. We'll find out more once we get inside the house. Until we can legally do that and assess the situation, we have no choice but to let Ken go."

"What's your next step?"

"We've set up a surveillance team to keep watch over the house where Ken alleged Megan had gone to a private home showing. We're waiting for a search warrant so we can legally enter the premises."

His answer tested Michael's patience and he blurted, "Why not go in now? What if Megan is inside the house? What if she's hurt?"

The detective dismissed his questions with a wave. "You know better than that. We need a warrant to get inside."

Michael relented, aware that he was letting his emotions get the better of him. "What about the home security systems in bordering homes?"

"The houses in that area were built more than a century ago. Handed down from generation to generation. Old money. With the increase in break-ins lately, several homeowners admitted they purchased security alarm systems, but not all were equipped with outdoor cameras. No leads there so far."

Another unresolved matter bothered Michael. "Do you have any news about the identity of the body discovered in the trunk of Megan's car?"

Esposito shook his head. "We haven't received the autopsy reports."

Michael needed the answer to another question niggling at the back of his mind. "Did Ken Reilly say why he met Megan at the Parkhurst Street address in the first place?"

"He'd overheard Brett Paquette talking to you over the phone about meeting to view a house on Hillside Avenue that evening. Ken was instructed to give Megan the address on Parkhurst Street for an earlier viewing and intercept her there before leading her to the open house viewing."

"Who instructed him?"

"The owner's niece."

"All that running around doesn't make sense. Why would Ken lead Megan to the Parkhurst Street address, then bring her to the other house—the so-called niece's place—for the showing? Something doesn't add up."

"To be clear, Megan drove her own car to the showing voluntarily. It's what happened afterward that's puzzling."

"Not to me," Michael said. "Ken threw Megan to the wolves. He could have been in on it." Another detail surfaced. "How did he get Megan's phone number anyway?"

"From your file at MRG, I suppose."

"They only have *my* phone number on file."

Esposito scribbled a note. "I'll ask Ken about it."

"That's more proof why I don't trust the guy."

"Rest assured that we're keeping him under surveillance. That's partly why we let him go."

"Partly? What's the other reason?"

"If Ken played a role in Megan's kidnapping, it's crucial that we discover who else is in on it. We hope he'll lead us to the big fish. The key person behind the plot."

Michael appreciated the detective's strategy. They were finally thinking along the same lines. "About the woman who Ken claimed duped him… He must have been communicating with her for some time."

"We asked to see his cell phone and he complied. We traced the woman's number to a disposable phone. Dead end."

"Do you have a description of her?"

"About five feet tall. Petite frame and blonde."

Michael sat upright. "It's a long shot, but I might have seen her the night Megan vanished." He recounted how a blonde woman had flirted with him at an all-night store, then he gave the detective the name and location of the place.

Esposito wrote the details in his notebook. "We'll examine the store's surveillance system video. It could provide a vital lead to her identity."

There was another woman Michael wanted to discuss with him. "I heard that Jane Barlow escaped from jail."

"I saw the bulletin. The police haven't found her yet."

"She could be here in Montreal."

The detective's eyes flickered. "You suspect she's linked to Megan's kidnapping?"

"It's possible. As far as prime suspects go, I learned through personal experience to never underestimate Jane."

"I thought Gabe Rivard was your number one suspect."

"Where a hit on me is concerned, yes, because the guy is a killer. But his MO doesn't match up with planning an elaborate kidnapping. Jane, on the other hand, is a formidable schemer and manipulator."

"You just chucked another potential killer into the mix," the detective pointed out.

"It wouldn't be the first time Jane hired an ex-con to do her dirty work," Michael said. "She met a bunch of them through her job as a paralegal. Sure, Rivard has a vendetta against me, but Jane might have activated the hit."

"It's conceivable. They both want revenge against you. On the other hand, it could be a coincidence."

"What do you mean?"

"One suspect might be behind the attack on you at the condo and another behind Megan's disappearance. So far, we have no evidence that either Jane Barlow or Gabe Rivard is involved in the shooting at the condo or Megan's abduction. Nor do we have proof they're working together."

"Are you any closer to finding Rivard?"

"No."

"Maybe the blonde mystery woman has a connection to him or Jane," Michael suggested.

Esposito flipped to a new page in his notebook. "I'll call the women's prison in Quebec where Jane was serving time. Maybe she had female friends on the inside who have since been released."

Michael moved on to another topic. "That arrangement Ken had with the mystery woman to bring Megan to her so-called aunt's house..."

"What about it?"

"You said it was an open house viewing. Did Ken mention if other potential buyers were present?"

"Yes, there were others. At one point, he received a phone call from the niece and left. That was the last he saw of Megan."

"What? Wasn't he was supposed to try to close the deal to get extra money? He left Megan there. That's unbelievable!"

"Ken claims the owner's niece told him to take the money she'd left him in an envelope and leave immediately."

Michael didn't hold back. "Is that why you think he's a patsy in all this? Give me a break."

The detective pursed his lips in annoyance. "Look, we have nothing on Ken to link him to Megan's disappearance. We can't charge him for simply accepting money from a woman."

"So that's it?"

"For now, yes." Esposito stood up. "Thanks for stopping by, Michael. I'll keep you in the loop if we find out anything more."

Michael left the station, his mood as blustery as the autumn wind blowing down his neck. If Esposito couldn't find out more about Ken Reilly, he knew exactly who could.

Time was running out and he needed answers. Now.

Brett led him into a meeting room at MRG. "The police were here earlier. Any news on Megan?"

"They cops are working on it," Michael said, noncommittal.

Brett took a seat at the conference table and motioned for Michael to do the same. "They interviewed Ken Reilly and me. When MRG owners found out that Ken might be involved in Megan's disappearance, they fired him on the spot."

"The cops haven't charged him with a crime," Michael said, not in defense of the man but merely stating the obvious.

"It doesn't matter. It's about the optics. Once word gets out, it'll make the agency look bad in the eyes of the public."

"Did Ken try to defend himself?"

"No. He packed up his things and left. It was for the best."

"What do you mean?"

"He wasn't cut out for the job."

"Oh?"

"I told you about him before," Brett said. "How he tried to steal other agents' sales by snooping into their listings. How he'd pop up at their open house showings and hand out his business card to their clients to solicit them."

"Sounds like he had money problems," Michael said.

"As far as I know, he never asked anyone at MRG for a handout. He got phone calls from bill collectors, though."

"Do you know if he was moonlighting?"

"Working a second job?" Brett raised an eyebrow. "I doubt it. He was a gambler. His only passion was get-rich-quick schemes. Even when he'd lose large sums of money, it didn't seem to bother him. He'd even brag about it. Ironically, he had a trust issue with his clients. He secretly recorded his conversations with them. Can you imagine?"

Michael found it interesting but said nothing.

"But now... With his questionable connection to Megan's disappearance..." Brett shrugged. "What more can I say? This is a new low, even for Ken. Why would he get involved in something as horrendous as—" He stopped. "I'm sorry. I don't mean to sound trite."

"Can you tell me anything about his personal life? Is he married?"

"He's single. He dated the same girl for a while—nothing serious. He's a fantastic uncle to his two nephews. He takes them to hockey and baseball games, gives them expensive gifts at Christmas, on their birthdays...stuff like that."

"Do you know anything more about him that might help me find Megan?"

Brett blinked, surprised. "I don't know how to answer that."

"Here's an easier question," Michael said. "Where does Ken live?"

"Sorry. There's no way I can give you that information."

"Then I have no choice. I'll find him myself. Thanks for your time." He rose from his chair.

Brett stood up and grabbed his arm. "Don't do this, Michael. It's best to let the police handle the investigation."

Michael jerked out of his grasp. "Not when it comes to finding Megan alive. Every second counts."

"Listen to yourself. You can't go off like this. Half-crazed."

"Says who?" Michael stormed out.

24

MICHAEL

Friday afternoon

They hadn't yet removed Ken Reilly's personal cell phone number from the MRG website.

Sitting in his condo living room, Michael took note of the number and placed the call. There was no answer. After the voice recording, he left a message.

His phone rang seconds later. But it wasn't Ken.

"Is this Michael Elliott?" An elderly woman's voice came across the line.

"Yes," he said. "Who's calling?"

"We met the other day on the street. My name is Dorothy. You gave me your business card."

Michael's pulse raced. Maybe she was calling to say that someone had seen Megan in the neighborhood. "Yes, Dorothy, I remember you."

"I'm calling to tell you that something strange happened next door at Helen's house yesterday."

Michael hid his disappointment. "What happened?"

"I was walking Ginger when I saw a huge man in the garage.

He was loading boxes into the back of an SUV parked there. My eyesight isn't so great, and it was pouring rain, but I saw him get into the back seat. Three women got into the vehicle too. One of the women stopped and waved at me before she got in."

"Was it Helen, your neighbor?"

"No, it was a much younger woman. Not the short, blonde-haired woman who had answered the door when I rang asking about Helen. Another one."

Short blonde? Michael sprang to his feet. "Can you describe the other woman? The one who waved at you."

"I couldn't see her face too well," Dorothy said. "She had a scarf wrapped around part of her head and across her mouth, which I found quite peculiar."

"Did you notice anything else? The color of her hair?"

"Her hair was dark. A little on the auburn side. It could have been the way the light in the garage hit it."

Megan!

Michael grabbed his jacket and car keys. "Did she say anything to you?"

"No, but she waved at me," Dorothy said. "It was a small wave—like her fingers wiggling. Her hands were tucked under a piece of clothing she was holding."

He had to assume that Megan had been in some kind of restraints. "Did you wave back?"

"I couldn't. I was holding an umbrella in one hand and a dog leash in the other."

Phone in hand, Michael hastened out the door and down the four flights of stairs to the ground level. "What happened afterward?"

"The blonde-haired woman and the one who waved at me got into the SUV. The driver—another woman—backed out of the garage, and they left."

"Can you describe the driver?"

"No, it was raining too hard," Dorothy said. "And the SUV windows were tinted."

"What time did they leave?"

"I don't know exactly. It was late evening. I would have called you sooner, but I misplaced your business card. I found it moments ago."

Damn! Megan had to be miles away by now.

Dorothy went on. "I don't believe those people were house sitting for Helen. They wouldn't have left before she returned from her trip." She sighed. "I'm deluding myself. Something awful has happened to Helen." Her voice trembled.

Michael reached the lobby and stopped. It was raining hard —like the night before. "Please hold on a moment, Dorothy," he said into the phone. He checked the street for any conspicuous vehicles, then ran to the parking lot and slid behind the wheel of his car. He switched his phone to hands-free. Dreading that Dorothy was right about her neighbor's fate, he asked her, "Have you contacted the police?"

"Yes, an hour ago. I was too afraid to call them sooner. I thought the people next door would return at any moment. I'm old and I live alone, you see. In any case, Detective Sergeant Esposito was quite considerate."

Esposito. It made sense. Michael sped down the street and took a sharp right at the corner. "What did he say?"

"He said he would come right over to talk to me and drop by Helen's property. In fact, he left my home moments ago. Let me see." There was a crackling of slats as she peered through the blinds. "Yes, two police cars, an ambulance, and a white truck are still parked out front."

"Thank you, Dorothy." Michael ended the call and drove to Parkvale Street.

Esposito's search warrant had come through. It had to be the same house the detective had placed under surveillance. The house where Ken said he'd left Megan. It was too much of a coincidence to be otherwise.

Michael had been standing in front of that same house only days ago. How had it all escaped him?

Dorothy was the lucky break he'd been waiting for. She'd seen a man and three women get in an SUV.

The third woman in the car—the driver. Was it Jane? If so, how would Ken Reilly be connected to someone like her?

The common link so far was the petite blonde who Ken claimed he knew. Michael had a hunch it was the same woman who'd smiled at him at the all-night store.

And who was that huge guy Dorothy had mentioned? It definitely wasn't Rivard. He was short and thin.

How were these other people connected to Jane?

Michael had all the pieces, but they just didn't fit.

He parked behind the ambulance and the forensics truck in front of Dorothy's house. Two police cruisers were positioned further up, their red and blue lightbars reflecting off the windows of surrounding houses.

He surveyed the premises. Police tape cordoned off the property on Parkvale Street, and law enforcement activity on the premises was evident. Although the rain had tapered to a light drizzle, it would hinder their progress outdoors.

He hardly had time to step out of his car before Esposito dashed out of the Parkvale home and made a beeline for him. He anticipated a barrage of questions from him.

The detective adjusted the collar of his overcoat. "How did you know to come here?"

"I have my sources," Michael said, tucking his hands in his jacket. "Any trace of Megan?"

"You should know better than to ask me that."

Michael glared at him. "I have every right to ask you that."

Esposito raised his hands in a gesture of placation. "Look, I know how personal this case is for you, so I'll share this much. No bodies were found inside. There's some blood spatter, but it could belong to the owner."

Michael was somewhat relieved. There was hope Megan was still alive.

The detective's attention wandered. "It's a large property,

but forensics should be finished gathering fingerprints and other evidence by tomorrow morning. Weather permitting, they'll complete their search outdoors by then too."

"Megan's fingerprints are on file for elimination purposes. In case."

"I know. I've already advised forensics." He paused. "By the way, we received the preliminary autopsy results for the body discovered in Megan's car."

"And?" Michael held his breath.

"It wasn't Megan."

Michael exhaled. It increased the chances that she could have been one of the women Dorothy saw getting in the SUV. "Do you know the victim's identity?"

"Yes. She was the owner of this house. Autopsy reports suggest that her body was dumped in Megan's car before the perpetrators drove off. She was strangled."

"No one deserves to die like that." Michael reflected on the older woman's fate.

"Oddly enough, we received our best tip today from an elderly woman who lives next door." The detective raised a thumb to indicate the house behind him.

Dorothy's house, Michael thought.

"We missed interviewing her the first time around. She was out walking her dog."

"So she led you to the house where Megan was held captive."

"We have no solid proof that Megan has been here so far." Esposito's words were guarded. "Simply put, the neighbor had her own reasons for calling us."

Michael considered how destiny had intervened when he'd circled the block and met Dorothy the other day. He decided to be upfront about what she'd told him regarding the SUV and the four occupants she'd seen in her neighbor's garage, including her encounters with the blonde woman.

It wasn't as if Esposito didn't already have Dorothy's witness statement. It was rather that Michael wanted to show him he was willing to collaborate in the investigation.

Esposito's eyes flickered after Michael finished his account. "It explains why you popped up here. I don't want to raise your hopes, but yes, Megan might be one of the people Dorothy saw."

"Maybe she can help to identify the blonde woman."

"Maybe. As for the others, she couldn't see them clearly through the rain."

Michael clenched his fists inside his pockets. "I wished I'd have known about this house sooner. I could kick myself for not checking it further."

"You couldn't have known at the time. No one could."

Michael moved on. "Any news on Gabe Rivard?"

Esposito nodded so-so. "Officers picked him up at a local tavern, but he's not talking. No trace of his vehicle either. No surprise, given the way these felons cover their tracks."

"What about Jane Barlow?"

"A correctional officer at the prison briefed me about her. She's quite a number. She instigated a fight so she could get medical care outside the prison. Then she slipped past the guards at the hospital and walked right out."

Old news, Michael thought. "Jane is delusional—and dangerous. She won't let anything stop her from getting what she wants."

The detective glanced down, tapped a pebble with his foot. "I've considered your theory about her. How she could have organized an elaborate escape plan *and* a kidnapping long before she arranged that prison fight." He focused on Michael. "If you're right, she could have it in for Megan big time."

"It's me she's after. She's using Megan as bait to reel me in."

"Authorities are working around the clock to track Jane down. They'll send me information if something develops. I'll keep in touch." He went back inside Helen's house.

Michael slid into the driver's seat. He felt encouraged after his meeting with Esposito. At least they were on the same page.

He'd driven several blocks when his phone rang. The display read Unknown Caller. A lead from an informant? He steered the car into a parking space on the street and answered.

Jane's words cut into him like a serrated knife. "I have Megan. You have forty-eight hours to find her. Come alone."

The line went dead.

25

────────

JANE

Friday night

Jane gazed out of the cabin window at the moonlight glistening on the lake. It reminded her of the carefree nights she'd spent in abandoned bliss with Michael that magical summer years ago.

Sharing romantic walks under the spell of a full moon. Talking about anything and everything. Enjoying each other's company in bed—and then some. Oh yes, he was the right man for her from the start.

It shattered her world when he broke off their relationship because of a silly excuse—something clichéd about a conflict of interest regarding a court case. So what if they were working for opposing legal teams? She promised him she wouldn't tell anyone about their relationship. But Michael didn't want to play along. Poor sport.

He said it was over between them, but then he started dating Megan—a married woman—weeks later. Jane tried to win him back, but Megan kept interfering with her plans, evoking Michael's sympathy for her after she lost her husband.

Then there was the murder trial. Jane had sworn in court that the deaths of Megan's husband and his girlfriend were accidental, but nobody believed her. Megan testified against her and so did Michael. It wasn't his fault—he didn't have a choice. It was Megan's fault. She had brainwashed him into believing she was an innocent victim, and then she seduced him.

But that was all in the past. Jane knew what she had to do. She had to get rid of Megan once and for all.

Soon she would release Michael from the guilt trip Megan had dumped on him all these years. He would be hers and hers alone. Nothing would separate them again.

That is, if he managed to survive until then.

Jane had searched online the other night for news about her escape from the hospital. All she found were articles from reporters who made no reference to her ingenious getaway plan.

A piece about a shooting at a Montreal condo had caught her attention. She viewed the accompanying video clip and zoomed in on a frame showing people standing near the entrance. Although the image was grainy, she recognized someone. Michael. His arms were bloody.

Was he was involved in the incident somehow? Had he been the intended target? If so, how fortunate that he'd escaped a premature death. Her intricate plan would have been all for nothing.

Michael had lots of enemies—revengeful ex-convicts who wanted to even the score. But she wasn't one of them. She wouldn't hurt Michael.

All the same, the police wouldn't be able to connect her to the incident. It wasn't because they didn't think she was up for the task. She was an outstanding shot. It was rather that not many people were aware of her particular skill.

In fact, only one person was. Her father.

He'd taught her how to use a hunting rifle and track deer when she was fifteen years old. She needed to protect herself, he said. She'd learned how to shoot even before her first date with that boy in high school who made unwanted advances toward her. She was tempted to use that pushy teen for target practice, but lucky for him, she changed her mind. She hitched a ride into town with a friend and went shoplifting instead.

No, shooting her victims wasn't her chosen *modus operandi.* Too messy. Her retaliation techniques were much more refined, like sending one-word text messages to Michael. *Vengeance.* It was solely meant as a forewarning of things to come, of course, and not a direct threat to him. He would stumble upon her punitive MO soon enough.

That remarkable cubbyhole in the cabin was so appropriate for what she'd planned for Megan. Exceptional service came at a price, and her father's carpenter friend had been worth every penny.

When she called Michael earlier, she'd longed to hear his voice and talk to him, but she had to keep her message brief. "I have Megan," she'd said to him. "You have forty-eight hours to find her. Come alone." She would have given anything to see the astonished look on his face. No need to rush, she reminded herself. There would be other opportunities later.

After she'd turned off the phone, she handed it to Lardo and told him to ditch it. The big guy had smashed it and tossed it deep in the woods where no one would find it. It would be impossible to trace the burner phone back to her.

Noises on the main floor diverted her attention. There was a more pressing problem: Megan. She had to deal with her.

Timing was crucial to Jane's plan. She had to carry out her psychological method of torture in finely measured steps. It was a technique she'd learned as a paralegal.

The court case had involved a member of the armed forces who'd returned from the war in Afghanistan. Enemy troops had caught and tortured him before rescuers could reach him. Loud, heavy metal music and strobe lights for days on end in a confined room with white walls had driven him over the edge.

Jane envisioned the predictable consequences of her simple but effective plan. Megan's brain would start to slide. Her thinking process would slow down. Finally, her will would break. She might even create an alternate reality to cope with the stress. What a superb coup it would be!

The general idea of this mode of torture was to get prisoners to break down and talk, but she definitely didn't need Megan to talk. She'd heard enough talk from that woman. She'd like nothing better that to shut her up for good.

Megan was to blame for her incarceration. No one else. Nothing would give her more gratification than to see her suffer. It would compensate for the years she had to put up with horrible food, pestering jail mates, and bullying guards. Yes, she wanted to see Megan squirm and snivel at her feet while she begged for her life.

All in all, Jane couldn't complain. Her torture strategy had indicated a promising start. Tiny and Lardo had followed her instructions and fed Megan less and less every day since she was kidnapped. How long ago was that? Three or four days? It was enough time to weaken her physically, if not emotionally.

The exception was that silly dash Megan had attempted on the highway. Her resilience and determination were surprising, if not unproductive. It wouldn't happen again. Jane would make sure of it. She would drug Megan's water and food to keep her spaced out. She would put her in her own orbit, as it were.

Jane laughed quietly.

A couple more days of raucous music and flashing lights would break Megan down and have her wondering what her name was. By the time Michael found her—and Jane was totally confident that he would—Megan would be a vegetable.

Hell, she'd be such a mess that Michael wouldn't want her back. Ever.

26

MICHAEL

Saturday morning

Esposito was Michael's first caller early Saturday morning. Although he welcomed his call, hearing the detective's voice caused his pulse rate to rise like no jog around the block could accomplish. "Any news about Megan?"

"No," Esposito said. "Among other things, I'm calling to find out if you got any more calls from Jane Barlow."

"I doubt she'll call back." Michael's tone was bleak. "She defined her deadline and I've started the countdown. We have less than forty hours to find Megan."

"Any more *vengeance* messages?"

"No, which tells me Jane was probably sending them too. It's a long shot, but did you have any luck in tracing the phone number I gave you?"

"No. It was a disposable phone. Jane must have bought a supply of them with that purpose in mind." There was a discernible pause before he went on. "Forensics located a set of fingerprints on a kitchen chair in the house on Parkvale Street.

We ran them through police records and came up with a name. Tanya Cordi. She goes by the nickname Tiny."

"I don't recognize either names," Michael said. "Got a description?"

"She's about five feet tall," Esposito said. "Small build. Blonde hair. Fits the description that you and another witness gave us."

The woman he'd seen at the all-night store. "Can you send me a photo?"

"It's on its way."

"What did Tiny serve time for?"

"Illegal drug possession and trafficking."

"When was she released?"

"Several months ago," Esposito said. "She served time in the same prison as Jane Barlow. Your hunch about their connection could be bang on."

"Anything about the big guy who rode off in the SUV with them?"

The detective drew a sigh. "Nothing. It's possible he doesn't have a criminal record. Forensics didn't find any prints in the house matching Jane's either."

"She must have worn plastic gloves the whole time," Michael said. "Even in the shower."

Esposito chuckled.

"I'm serious. You have no idea how manipulative she is."

"I do now." Esposito's tone grew more somber. "Forensics ran into another problem. Renovations had been underway in the basement of the Parkvale Street home, which means more fingerprints have to be eliminated."

Dorothy had said something about painters working next door. "The next-door neighbor might know how to reach the painting crew."

"Thanks, but we've got that covered."

"Any other leads?"

"We're running a description of the SUV through local auto rentals. Nothing so far."

"Time is running out." Michael's tone reflected urgency. "We need to find evidence that could lead to where they've taken Megan."

"Don't go and do anything rash," Esposito warned him. "Let us handle this. Contact me if you hear from Jane again." He ended the call.

Michael accessed the photo the detective had sent him. The blonde was the same woman he'd seen at the local all-night store. He sent Esposito a reply confirming it.

Tiny. The woman must have followed Megan and him around town. It was the only way she could have known they were house hunting. The prior meeting at the Parkhurst Street home that evening was a setup. Tiny had instructed Ken Reilly to go there, knowing that a security system video would cast doubts on Megan's relationship with Michael.

To think Esposito had almost bought it.

He'd bet Tiny was the same woman who'd introduced herself to Dorothy as her neighbor's niece. The same short blonde Dorothy had seen in the garage.

The pieces were starting to fall into place.

Except for Ken. The real estate agent didn't quite fit into Jane's tightly knit group. He didn't strike him as the sort of guy to hang around with the likes of Gabe Rivard either.

But Michael had already eliminated Rivard as a suspect in Megan's kidnapping, hadn't he?

Which left Tiny and the huge guy as the other links to Ken. And he already had proof that Tiny was part of Jane's scheme.

A strategy slowly formed in Michael's thoughts.

How could he get Ken to confess and admit he knew Tiny's real name? That she had a criminal record?

After Megan's disappearance hit the news, the guy must have been terrified within inches of his life. If so, was it the reason he'd given the cops a fake name for Tiny?

Either Ken was covering up for Tiny or he was protecting himself from potential criminal repercussions. If the latter, had Ken suspected that Tiny was up to no good when she asked him to intercept Megan on Parkhurst Street? He hadn't done it for free. Was money the only motive that had compelled him to be such a snake?

Michael brewed a pot of coffee. He filled a mug and opened up his laptop where he'd kept notes since the evening Megan had vanished. Now that he had a better picture of who was involved, he could devise a solid plan to ensnare them.

He reviewed his notes:

- The testimony from the nanny at the Parkhurst Street house about Megan meeting Ken...
- Ken's validation that Tiny asked him to redirect Megan to a house viewing on Parkvale Street, how Tiny paid him a load of cash for it...
- Tiny lied to Ken about privately selling the house on behalf of her dead aunt, how Ken had—or hadn't—checked the actual ownership of the Parkvale house before he agreed to get involved...
- Brett's account of Ken's intrusion in other real estate agents' deals, how Ken eavesdropped on agents' conversations, how Ken didn't trust his own clients and recorded his conversations with them...
- Esposito's validation that Tiny had served time in the same jail as Jane, that Tiny's fingerprints were found in the house on Parkvale Street...
- Dorothy's eyewitness account of a young woman who could have been Megan, her account of three other people—including a short blonde, a huge guy, and another woman (Jane?)—driving away from Helen's house in a black SUV...
- Jane's phone call confirming she had Megan...

Michael examined every fragment of information. What stuck out was that several people had taken part in Megan's kidnapping. Jane had created an elaborate plan—one that demanded the trust and loyalty of these people so that it would succeed.

Trust.

Could anyone be trusted today? Even two-faced Ken Reilly was incapable of trusting his own clients and made it a practice to record their conversations.

Hold on. Recordings? Was Michael onto something? Was there a chance that Ken had recorded his conversation with Tiny about selling the Parkvale Street house?

He accessed the contact list on his phone. Ken hadn't returned his first call, so Michael left him another message.

Next on his list was Dorothy. Although Esposito would track down the people working on the home renovations next door, something urged Michael to call her.

He was relieved when she picked up the phone. Without mentioning Esposito or the police, he asked, "Dorothy, would you have the name of the painter you recommended to Helen?"

"Yes," Dorothy said. A shuffling of papers ensued. "Here it is. His name is Enrico. He owns a renovation business." She gave him the phone number. "He's a hard-working young man. Tell him I sent you."

Michael called Enrico and arranged to meet with him at his downtown apartment right away. He had a hunch, and he was counting on the painter to back it up.

Enrico had morphed his one-room apartment into a melting pot of undertakings. From an old-fashioned percolator concocting delicious-smelling coffee to the painting of a young woman on an easel to four pots of something dubious, tall, and green growing by the window, Enrico liked to surround himself with productive activities.

"I am comfortable in my own skin and enjoy creating new things," Enrico said, serving Michael coffee in a fancy porcelain cup. "But I make the exception for exquisite hand-me-downs, like this fine set of porcelain cups and saucers my grandmother sent me from Italy."

Michael took a sip. "Excellent coffee." He meant it. "You're quite the artist." He pointed to the canvas on an easel.

"Thank you. I enjoy it a lot." Enrico took a seat across from him at the small round table. "You said Dorothy sent you. Are you here to request a portrait?"

"I'd like to talk about something else before." Michael sipped more coffee. "I understand you were hired by Helen, Dorothy's neighbor, to paint her basement."

Enrico frowned. "I worked for a week and didn't get paid. It's hard to run a business these days."

"I understand that Helen's niece was living at the house for a while."

"I only saw her once. She opened the door one morning and told me to leave and not come back."

"You didn't finish the job?"

"No. I told her I wanted to finish, but she insisted."

"Did she say why?"

"She said her aunt had passed away suddenly and that she was selling the house. I wanted to get paid and asked her for the money. When she said she couldn't pay me right away, I didn't argue. Especially not with that huge guy standing next to her."

"Can you describe him?"

"I'll do better. I'll draw him for you." Enrico reached for a charcoal pencil and a drawing pad.

Michael watched as the artist rapidly sketched the man that Dorothy had seen get in the SUV that night.

When Enrico had finished, he tore off the sheet and handed it to him.

Michael shuddered inwardly as he took note of the beady eyes set within a round unshaven face and dark straight hair that reached chin level. "How tall was the man?"

"About six foot five. He was hairy and massive and had gigantic hands. I value my life, so I won't be going back there to claim my payment." He let out a nervous laugh.

"Can I keep this sketch?"

"Yes."

A promising lead. Michael dug out two fifty-dollar bills. "Thank you. I appreciate your help."

Enrico accepted the bills and smiled. "Consider this a down payment on a future painting I will do for you."

Michael stepped out of Enrico's apartment building with one thought on his mind: How could anyone expect Megan to get away from that hefty monster working for Jane?

At least he knew what the guy looked like now. He'd have to equip himself properly in case he ever bumped into him.

After he returned to his car, he took a photo of Enrico's drawing and sent it to Esposito with a message: This is a sketch of the big guy who helped kidnap Megan. Obtained from a very reliable source.

He was about to drive away when his phone buzzed. He accessed the message. It read: *Vengeance.*

27

MICHAEL

Saturday morning

When Ken agreed to meet with him at a local coffee shop on Sherbrooke Street, Michael's spirits soared. Maybe the guy wanted to divulge facts that he didn't feel comfortable sharing with the cops. Or maybe he was looking for an excuse to get Michael on his side.

"Sorry I didn't get back to you sooner," Ken said, slipping into the booth. "I haven't been sleeping well these days."

"Makes two of us." Sarcasm filtered through Michael's voice.

Were the dark circles under Ken's eyes proof of his unrest? Maybe a guilty conscience was preventing him from getting a good night's sleep.

Awareness flowed over Ken's face. "I guess the cops told you I brought Megan to a house showing. I unknowingly put her in trouble and want to help you in any way I can."

Unknowingly? Sheer willpower prevented Michael from reaching across the table and strangling Ken with his own tie. The guy was lucky the waitress came by and filled their cups with coffee.

"In my line of business, it's hard to know who to trust." Ken drank some coffee. "I've learned the hard way that I need to protect myself from people who might be trying to take advantage of me."

"It didn't stop you from doing the same."

"What do you mean?"

Michael didn't hold back. "You took advantage of Megan's trust in you. Now she's missing. Or worse."

Ken loosened his tie. "You have no idea how terrible I feel... how stressed I am about what happened."

"Try me."

"Sorry, I didn't mean to offend you. That's why I'm here. I want to apologize for my mistake. I want to try to make it right."

Michael wasn't convinced. He'd need more tangible proof of Ken's sudden change of heart. "You said on the phone that you had information for me."

"Yes." Ken retrieved a flash drive from the inside pocket of his jacket and placed it on the table. "This copy is for you."

"What's on it?"

"Two conversations I had with Tiny, the woman who asked me to bring Megan to the house showing on Parkvale Street. Her real name is Tanya Cordi."

Michael didn't let on that he already had that information. "How do you know her?"

"I met her years ago at a party. We dated a few times...kept in touch now and again."

"How did you get mixed up with the house on Parkvale Street?" Again, he wanted to hear the answer directly from Ken, even though he'd already heard it from Esposito.

"Tiny told me it belonged to her aunt who had passed away. She asked me to sell it privately to a select group of interested buyers."

"Why did you think Megan was an interested buyer?"

"I didn't. Tiny mentioned her name—and yours. She said you were old friends who wanted to buy a house in the area."

"We don't know her," Michael said. "How did she find out we were working with an agent at MRG?"

Ken shifted in his seat. "I overheard conversations between you and Brett about house showings in the same area. When Tiny called, I accessed your file to get Megan's phone number."

Aha! A slip-up. "For the record, Brett doesn't have Megan's phone number on file."

"Oh. I guess Tiny got it from someone else."

Another puzzle for Michael to solve. He went on. "Why did you arrange to meet Megan at an earlier time on Parkhurst Street?"

"How did you know about that?"

"Just answer the question."

Ken scowled. "Hey, I was following Tiny's instructions. She told me it was sort of a game, that I was to give Megan flowers and pretend I'd screwed up the address. Then I was to bring her to the other house on Parkvale Street for the private showing instead."

"And you didn't question her reasons behind the setup on Parkhurst Street?"

"Like I told you, Tiny said it was a game. I didn't think anyone would get hurt."

Michael felt his muscles tighten but crushed the urge to hurt Ken. "Why did you walk out on Megan at the showing?"

"Tiny told me she hadn't seen Megan in years, that it would be a surprise reunion between old friends. She phoned me minutes after we entered the house and told me to make up an excuse to leave. She said she had a better chance of selling the house to Megan personally because she knew her. She promised to call me as soon as the deal went through."

"Why didn't Tiny call Megan directly?"

"It could have been part of the surprise." Ken drank more coffee, then fidgeted with his cup. "I was sure Megan would go to the house showing on Hillside Avenue afterward. I had no idea someone would kidnap her. It was never part of the deal."

"Did the cops tell you the owner wasn't Tiny's aunt?"

Ken lowered his head. "Yes, and I feel horrible about that."

Michael clenched his jaw. "You're a professional real estate agent. Didn't you verify the ownership of the house before you agreed to sell it?"

Ken raised his chin. "Hey, why would I burden myself with the paperwork if the deal eventually fell through?"

You lazy scumbag, Michael thought. Anger surged inside him, and he struggled to remain focused. "Will Tiny stay in touch with you?"

"I don't know. She mentioned she was going out of town for a while."

"Did she say where?"

"No."

One name in particular on Michael's suspect list jarred his memory. "Who else is involved in Megan's kidnapping?"

"How would I know?" The veins in Ken's neck protruded. "I already told you that I had no idea she was going to get kidnapped."

Could that part of Ken's admission be true? Michael picked up the flash drive. "What's recorded on this drive again?" He slid it in his jacket.

"The first conversation is with Tiny when she approached me to sell the house. We discussed the advance cash payment and what she wanted me to do to get Megan to the showing. The second conversation is where we set up a meeting time so I could deliver...um...stuff to her."

"What stuff?"

Ken shook his head. "You can listen to the recording later. I'm in enough trouble already."

"What stuff?" Michael's raised voice caught the attention of patrons at the booth beside them.

Ken leaned forward and whispered, "Drugs."

"You're a drug dealer too?"

"Hey, it's a tough world out there. I have to make a living."

Ken straightened up, an arrogant grin spreading across his face. "Anyway, you can't tell the cops about this. You told me our conversation would be confidential, that it's protected under journalistic privilege."

"True," Michael said, wishing it weren't. "What I did expect was your help in finding Megan."

"I told you everything I know. What more do you want?"

"Did you give a copy of the flash drive to the police?"

"No."

"Then do it. Make it right."

Ken gaped at him. "Are you nuts? If they hear the second recording, they'll arrest me for drug trafficking."

"You can try to work something out with them to redeem yourself." Michael suggested a way he could make that prospect materialize.

His meeting with Ken had impelled Michael to broaden his views as far as Jane's secret location was concerned. If it were true that Tiny was going out of town, it had to be an out-of-the-way place that Jane was familiar with and where she wouldn't be easily recognized.

The only other person who knew Jane as well as he did was his lawyer friend. After he settled in the living room, he called Dan. He was surprised when he immediately picked up.

"I took the day off," Dan said by way of explanation. "I was supposed to attend a conference in Toronto this weekend. I skipped out. It gave me a chance to catch up on paperwork."

"Paperwork? Is that how you take the day off?" Michael chuckled.

"Absolutely, but at a more leisurely pace." He paused. "Do you have any news about Megan?"

"No. I'm investigating some leads. I'm optimistic I'll find

her." Michael felt as if he were trying to convince himself rather than Dan.

"I wish there was a way I could help."

"Maybe you can. I need to find Jane. Did she ever mention her family and where they might be living?"

"Not that I can recall. You know how she was. She preferred to keep personal matters to herself."

"Would you have her original job application on file?"

"Let me see…" The sound of Dan's fingers tapping on the computer keyboard made its way over the line. "Yes. I have it. What specifically do you want to know, Michael?"

"A letter of reference. The name of a family member. An address or phone number."

"There's not much here. If I remember correctly, I hired Jane on the verbal approval of a trusted colleague. I didn't bother asking her for reference letters."

"Any names to contact in case of emergency?"

More tapping. "I have the name of a roommate Jane boarded with before I hired her."

"Can you give it to me?"

"It's highly irregular but—"

"It's only a personal reference, Dan, not legal information. It could mean the difference between finding Megan alive or dead."

"I hear you. I was going to add that current circumstances allow it. Her name is Amy Hill." Dan gave him her cell phone number. "I strongly advise you to pass this information on to the police."

"I'll check it out myself first," Michael said. "It might be a dead end. Besides, the idea of speaking to the cops might spook the roommate."

"All right. Then I won't try to talk you out of it."

After they'd said their goodbyes, Michael called Amy Hill. It would be a miracle if the woman's phone number was still active after all these years.

A young woman identified herself as "Amy" on the voice recording. He left a message.

Michael couldn't believe his good luck. How convenient that Jane's roommate had retained the same phone number. It occurred to him that Jane might have hung onto other phone numbers all this time too—namely Megan's and his. It would explain how Tiny was able to obtain Megan's number and pass it along to Ken.

He glanced at his watch. Only a matter of hours until Jane carried out her heinous threat.

Megan.

He imagined the physical suffering that Jane might have already inflicted on her. As he wrestled with the monstrous images, nausea swept over him. Of equal dread were Jane's psychological stunts, her twisted and demented ways.

Once a victim of her mind games, he'd experienced the emotional anguish she was capable of inflicting and the sadistic pleasure she derived from it. It was fortunate that he'd seen through her lies before it was too late.

Michael wasn't a shrink, but he knew that Megan's mental health had been stable enough to take her through some of the most challenging situations they'd encountered. Yet a part of him feared that Jane's sustained and brutal tactics might overwhelm her and crush her will.

He had to trust that his love for Megan would keep her safe. There was nothing more he could do but wait for Amy Hill to return his call. She was his last chance to reach Megan while she was still alive.

28

MICHAEL

Saturday afternoon

Amy Hill's tone was cautious. "If this is about Jane," she said to Michael when she returned his call, "I don't know anything. I have nothing more to say."

"Amy, wait!" He had to find a way to keep her on the line. "Please hear me out. This is about Megan Scott, the woman in my life. She's gone missing."

Her tone softened. "Oh...yeah. I saw the news report. Sorry to hear it. But what does it have to do with me?"

"Jane was your roommate years ago. Did you hear that she recently escaped from jail?"

"Yeah, and I've been terrified ever since."

"Why?"

"She was the roommate from hell. I was so happy when she went to work for a law firm and moved into another apartment. I moved too and didn't tell her where. I hope I never see her again."

"Did she ever talk to you about her family?"

"Jane rarely talked to me. She was too busy trying to land a rich husband. From what she did tell me, though, I learned you two were really close. No offense, but when she talked about you, it was mostly about the private stuff."

An embarrassing moment filled the silence as Michael imagined Jane bragging about her sexual exploits to Amy.

"That was her version of it." He brought the conversation back on track. "Did Jane ever mention the name of a city or town where her family lived?"

"Are you kidding? She wouldn't give me the time of day unless the conversation was about her latest male conquests or the court cases she helped win. There was one time though..." Amy hesitated. "She mentioned something about her family owning property outside Montreal. I don't remember the name of the town, but it reminded me of the singer, Adele."

"Was it Sainte-Adèle?"

"Yeah, that could be it."

Michael's heart beat with joy. "Terrific. Thanks, Amy."

"What's with all these questions about Jane's family?"

He had to tread carefully. "It might help the police track her down."

"Ha! You think she kidnapped Megan, don't you?"

"I didn't say that."

"You didn't have to. Nothing shocks me anymore about Jane. She was unpredictable. And cruel." She grew quiet. "Michael, can I ask you something?"

"What?"

"If you run into her, please don't tell her we've spoken. I still have nightmares about her."

"Your secret is safe with me."

Michael planned his next strategic move. If he wanted to put Jane Barlow back behind bars, he had to outfox her. The years she spent in jail talking to other inmates and picking up their tricks of the trade would have made her even more ruthless and conniving.

After his conversation with Amy, he searched online for the land registry office in Quebec that included the town of Sainte-Adèle. He didn't get far because the search not only required the owner's name but also the lot number of the property. He didn't have either.

Unable to access the information he needed, he filled a backpack with supplies and drove off. It would take him about an hour to reach the municipality north of Montreal.

He thought about notifying Esposito but dismissed the idea. At this point, he wasn't even sure he was on the right track. All he had to guide him was a gut feeling, and it wasn't enough to persuade the detective to take action. No, he was better off visiting the town on his own.

As soon as he hit the highway, the leaden sky opened up and it started to pour. The traffic was already heavy, owing to the early commuters heading up to the Laurentians for the weekend. The slowdown meant he'd reach his destination later than planned.

His phone rang. It was Esposito. Maybe he had news about Megan. Michael answered the call using his hands-free device.

"I just had a surprise visit from Ken Reilly," the detective said. "He offered valuable evidence regarding Megan's disappearance."

He had to be referring to Ken's recorded conversations with Tiny. "Like what?" Michael prompted him.

"Let me put it this way. He didn't resist when I suggested how he could help the police locate Megan."

"That's encouraging." The speed of the windshield wipers on Michael's car increased as the downpour amplified.

"It's noisy at your end. Are you going through a carwash or something?"

"No, I'm out for a drive."

Movement at the other end of the line. "In the rain?"

"It helps me to think. What were you saying about Ken?"

"Ken told us he kept in contact with Tanya Cordi—or Tiny," the detective said. "He consented to have us trace her next call when it comes in. If she's with Jane, we'll be able to close in on them and rescue Megan."

"It's a long shot," Michael said. "Tiny might ditch her phone right after she hangs up."

"Minor felons often make mistakes. A false sense of security might encourage her to keep using the same burner phone. It'll eventually do her in." He sounded confident.

"I'm counting on it."

"By the way, thanks for sending a sketch of the male suspect our way. We'll forward it to the media ASAP." He paused. "Enrico is quite the artist, isn't he?"

Michael discerned a smile in his tone. The detective—or a member of his investigative team—had evidently interviewed the painter too. "You bet."

~

As Michael took the exit for Sainte-Adèle, he noticed two other cars behind him. One turned off a side road and the other—a dark blue sedan—continued to tail him into town. He made a right turn and circled the block. So did the sedan.

Was someone following him?

He coasted along the main street of town and hastily slid into a parking spot perpendicular to a strip of shops. He checked his rearview mirror and saw the blue sedan drive by.

He surveyed the lineup of stores and settled on the coffee shop. Locals who knew one another by name met for coffee and conversation in cozy places like this. One of them might have information about the Barlow family. At the least, the coffee shop owner or staff might steer him in the right direction.

The downpour had lessened to a drizzle, but a chilly wind

forced him to raise the collar of his leather jacket. He hurried into the coffee shop and sat on a stool at the bar.

Two seats away, an elderly man hunched over the counter was speaking with a young waitress. Though French wasn't his forte, Michael managed to grasp the gist of their conversation. The man was complaining about the weather and how the humidity affected his arthritis.

"Sorry to hear that, Henri," the waitress said, her warm eyes resting on the man. "Let's hope the rain stops soon."

Henri muttered something about meeting his friends, then took out his wallet. He placed a ten-dollar bill on the counter and lumbered out.

The waitress walked over to Michael. "What can I get you?"

Michael dredged up his best French and ordered coffee and a grilled cheese sandwich. After she returned with his meal, he asked her if she knew anyone in town by the family name of Barlow.

"I've only been working here a few months," she said. "Henri—the man who just left here—he might know. He's lived in Sainte-Adèle all his life."

"Where can I find him?"

"At the bowling alley three doors down."

Michael decided his meal could wait. He stood up and reached for his wallet.

"You don't have to rush off," she said. "Henri will be there all afternoon. If he can't help you, one of his old pals might be able to."

The attendant asked Michael to wait by the counter while he strolled over to a group of seniors bowling in one of the lanes. "Henri, someone is here to see you." He stuck out a thumb toward Michael.

Henri squinted at Michael, then ambled toward him. "What can I do for you?" he asked in French.

Replying in French, Michael said, "I'm looking for someone. Would you happen to know a local resident by the name of Barlow?"

Henri replied in perfect English. "Yes, I know Barlow. Why are you looking for him?"

Relieved that he no longer had to struggle with words, Michael switched to English and made his pitch. "My wife and I want to buy a summer place here. I heard he had a property for sale."

Surprise washed over Henri's face. "It must be the property he owns by the lake. Darcy didn't tell me he had put it up for sale."

"It's a private sale," Michael said, fibbing again. "Is it far from here?"

"It's across the lake from Hôtel Le Chantecler. Can't miss it. A two-story log chalet with a private beach and an L-shaped wharf."

"How can I reach Darcy?"

"He lives at the local retirement home. It's been about five years now."

"Where's the home?"

Henri gave him directions. "At the rate my arthritis is acting up, I'll be joining him soon." He chuckled, then rubbed his chin. "Anyhow, I find it strange that he's selling that old property."

"Why?"

"It's been in the family for decades. I always thought..."

"What?"

"Nothing, really." Henri briefly turned away when one of his friends called out his name. "I have to go," he said to Michael. "Tell Darcy I said hello."

∾

Energized by the newfound information, Michael hastened to his car, his stride confident. It had stopped raining and the air smelled fresh with greenery. Traffic flowed freely. Pedestrians drifted along the sidewalk, peeking into shop windows. Under normal circumstances, it would have been an amazing spot to spend a relaxing weekend with Megan.

But nothing was normal about this day or the circumstances surrounding it. Megan was held hostage somewhere, and he had less than a day to find her. He had to reach her in time, or he wouldn't be able to live with himself.

He glanced up and down the street. There was no sign of the blue sedan that had tailed him earlier. It didn't mean anything. Maybe the guy had parked elsewhere and was walking about, blending in with the crowds. He'd have to remain vigilant.

The ten-minute drive to the retirement home felt longer. He blamed it on the anticipation rising inside him. Was Darcy Barlow a close relative of Jane or some distant uncle? He'd soon find out.

Nestled within a wooded area, the two-story red brick building looked more like a school than a retirement home. Michael announced his arrival at the front desk and asked for a visit with Darcy Barlow. A female attendant invited him to take a seat in the visitors' room while she went to get Darcy.

Pale walls and drab furniture were offset by two pots of hanging ferns that bordered a spacious window along the far side of the visitors' room. Two gray-haired women sat in armchairs flanking a fireplace and chatted quietly with each other. Other seniors played board games in an adjoining room where the noise vacillated between low murmurs and surges of loud chatter.

Michael attributed the slight medicinal scent in the air to a blend of products the elderly used for arthritic pain and breathing difficulties. The place was clean, which said a lot about the people running it.

The female attendant returned to say that Mr. Barlow was in a therapy session and would be done in half an hour. She asked Michael if he wanted to wait. He said yes.

He crossed the floor and chose a seat by the window and observed a landscape that autumn was preparing for winter. The abandoned chairs, picnic tables, and wilting gardens depressed him.

Strange how the bleak scenery reflected the void he felt in his life. He'd done some soul-searching lately and concluded that two things were missing from his life: Megan's trust in him and his parents' support of his career choice. The first was a work in progress. He had to prove to Megan that he was willing to sacrifice anything to be with her, that he'd be a loyal and loving husband. But to accomplish that, he had to find her.

And then there were his parents...

He'd rarely assessed things in the same light as his father—especially when it came to his job. They were miles apart in life goals and attitudes about money too. Michael didn't know what it would take to get through to him.

But he wouldn't stop trying. Keeping up the conversation with his parents was a crucial step. He pulled out his phone and made the call.

His father answered. "How are you, Michael?" His tone sounded conciliatory. Michael assumed that his mother had patched things up after their last conversation, as she often did. "Any word on Megan?"

There was no way Michael would share those specifics—not even with his father. Yet he felt he had to offer him something. "Keep this between us, Dad. The cops are making headway. And so am I."

"That sounds promising. Maybe we'll get some good news soon." An awkward moment of silence. "Your mother would like to talk to you. I'll put her on."

A rustling sound as the phone changed hands.

"Michael, any news about Megan?" His mother's voice was shaky.

He comforted her by repeating what he'd told his father.

"That's encouraging," she said. "We mustn't lose hope. I told your father how important it was to stay positive. Megan is a resourceful woman. She'll find a way to contact you."

"I'm counting the hours until I see her again." He was determined to make it happen. "Dad seems to be in a better mood."

"Well, we know you're going through a hard time," she said, bringing her diplomacy to the fore. "We're here for you—both of us—if you need anything. Anything at all."

"Thanks, Mom."

"When will we hear from you again?"

"After I find Megan." Michael noticed the attendant had returned. She was escorting an elderly man into the visitors' room. "I have to go, Mom. I promise I'll call you as soon as I hear anything."

The female attendant kept a slow pace beside a man who walked with a limp and used a cane. Wisps of gray hair topped his tall, slender frame. Stooped shoulders spoke of hard work— maybe decades as a carpenter or construction worker. He had the same sharp recognition in his eyes as Jane but with a mellowness in them that came with age and compassion.

There was no mistaking it.

Darcy was Jane's father.

29

MEGAN

Saturday afternoon

Michael entered the house with a smile on his face and a bouquet of beautiful summer blooms in his hand. I trimmed the stems, filled a vase with water, and organized the flowers just so. The arrangement worked perfectly as the centerpiece on the dining room table we'd recently purchased for our new home. Michael joined me in the kitchen and helped prepare dinner—chicken Parmesan— one of our favorites. He poured red wine into our glasses and—

"No, Michael, don't go! Don't leave me!"

I hardly recognized my own voice. It sounded different, feeble.

I moved my arms. The horrific reality was that I was still handcuffed and sitting on the floor in a soundproof closet.

I stretched my legs and felt muscle cramps down to my toes. How long had I been imprisoned in this confined space?

Wait. Something was different. It was quiet. And dark. No strobe lights were flashing. Was I imagining this too, or had there been a power failure?

The closet door slowly opened.

Tiny stood there, holding it slightly ajar. She said something over her shoulder, but I couldn't make out the words. They were muffled. The persistent ringing in my ears didn't help.

The muted sound of dishes crashing to the floor.

A woman shouting.

Tiny took a few steps to the right but remained in my line of sight. I took it as a sign that she wanted me to see something.

I edged closer to the narrow opening. As I peeked out, a refreshing breeze blew across my face.

Jane was standing in the kitchen. Anger contorted her features and she was yelling at Tiny and waving her hands in the air. She reached for a dish from the shelf and hurled it to the floor. She was clearly on a rampage, but I couldn't make out what she was saying.

Fear seized me. Had I lost part of my hearing because of the deafening music?

Jane picked up another plate and flung it across the room. It smashed into pieces at Tiny's feet and she screamed.

I pulled back, terrified. Curiosity prompted me to peek out the door again.

Jane kept yelling at Tiny. She rushed toward her, her fists pumping the air, her mouth twisted in anger.

Why was she so angry? Something must have set her off.

How odd. Jane had been so sociable the other day when she'd invited me to sit at the kitchen table and have coffee with her. She'd even offered me some chocolate almonds. They were delicious!

We'd sat for hours, chatting about the latest fashions and hairstyles, favorite movies and books, and other fun things. She'd been so friendly—not like the other Jane from long ago—the bad Jane. I preferred this new Jane.

So why had she put me back in the closet? What had I done to upset her? Had I done something wrong? Is that why she locked me up?

My stomach growled. My hands were cuffed.

This couldn't be right.

Jane was *not* nice.

Had I imagined the whole coffee chat with her? What was happening to me? Was I losing my mind?

I had to fight it. I had to stay in touch with reality, with what was happening around me.

I yawned to unclog my ears and heard a pop. Although my ears were ringing, I could hear Jane and Tiny better now.

"You forgot?" Jane stabbed a finger at Tiny's chest. "That's a poor excuse. The lights and music were supposed to stay on. You failed to do your job, Tiny."

"It's not my fault," Tiny said. "Lardo was stuffing his face in the kitchen, so I left the lights on downstairs. I was so tired, I must have turned off the closet switch by mistake instead of the hall switch before I went up to bed."

"You mean you were so stoned, you didn't know what you were doing."

"Maybe...I guess."

"What are you waiting for? Flip the switch on now!" Jane slammed the door shut.

Darkness encased me. "No!" I shouted.

The best part about having a cabin in the woods is that you can scream as loud as you want, and no one would hear you.

Raucous music pounded from the ceiling. It was real. I could feel it throbbing in the walls.

The strobe lights flashed. I shut my eyes tightly, but the lights were still visible, faster and faster, brighter and brighter.

Seamless white walls were closing in on me. Panic swept over me like a tidal wave, pumping fear through my veins. I was suffocating, gasping for air.

I tried to concentrate on Michael and envision a positive outcome, but the confined space, the agonizing lights, and the grating music were gaining on me.

Unbearable.

I could no longer lie to myself to stay alive. I'd cried all my tears. I was now drowning in self-pity, praying that someone would come and rescue me.

But how would anyone know where I was?

My guilt was eating away at me, telling me how careless I'd been. It was my fault alone that I'd ended up in this horrendous situation.

My world was roaring, spinning.

I waited for my brain to explode.

30

—————

JANE

Saturday afternoon

Most people were expendable.

Jane had discovered that years ago.

The only thing that kept people alive was how well they played the game.

Megan didn't know how to play the game. Miss goody-two-shoes did everything by the book. She wasn't a risk taker and that was no fun.

Michael, on the other hand, thrived on risk. He deserved an equally spirited female partner like Jane. Not that soppy excuse for a woman he felt he had to protect. To think that he wanted to buy a luxurious house in an affluent part of Montreal for her. What a waste!

Megan was pitiful. Jane had needed to execute her scheme ever so slowly to break the poor girl down, or she would have been dead by now. Yet nothing seemed to stifle that tramp's resolve to survive.

All the same, Jane congratulated herself. Her plan was working perfectly. All she needed was a few more hours. By the time Michael found Megan, she would be as useless to him as winter tires in Florida.

What had he seen in that woman to begin with? He was obviously confused—or brainwashed. Jane would fix things to make it right again. She would lure him out from under the spell of that schemer's fake charms and set him straight. She would show him what a perfect couple they made and how they could be together again. No one would keep them apart this time.

But first she had to take care of the loose ends. She'd spent too much time engineering her complex plans to see them evaporate because of silly blunders other people made. With that mindset in place, she acknowledged that people were only useful to her until they made mistakes.

Tiny had made a big one. While her loyal toady thought she was having a private conversation behind closed doors, Jane overheard her answering a phone call from her drug supplier. An inexcusable mistake! After all the warnings she'd given Tiny about giving out her phone number to strangers...

Sooner or later, one of Tiny's contacts would talk and spoil her plan. Someone always did. Then Jane would have to step in and fix things again.

Ken Reilly, Tiny's boyfriend and personal drug supplier, was someone who had the potential to ruin things for Jane. He'd followed Tiny's instructions, but it had cost Jane plenty to pay him off so he would keep his lips sealed.

There were no guarantees he wouldn't talk, though. She knew his type. He'd do anything for money, but he would just as easily blab to police investigators to save his own skin. He was another loose end she'd have to take care of. And she'd soon get the chance to do so.

She'd overheard Tiny on the phone making arrangements with Ken to come to the cabin to deliver a supply of drugs. Oh, how she'd wanted to tear into Tiny for having done that!

Only after she pondered her dilemma did she realize the

ironic stroke of luck that fate had sent her way. She could turn an unfavorable situation into a favorable one. How convenient that she didn't have to drive all the way back to Montreal to get rid of Ken! Tiny would deliver him right to her doorstep.

In the meantime, Jane would deal with Tiny. Of course, she'd have to delegate the task. It was too messy to handle such demeaning responsibilities herself. She'd ask Lardo to do it. He'd like that.

She laughed.

She saw the way Tiny ordered that gargantuan slob around, how Lardo restrained himself from ripping the pint-sized woman apart with his bare hands. He had no reason to refuse Jane's directive. Not that Lardo reasoned anything he did. That good-for-nothing dunce was as brainless as they came.

She laughed again.

The sketch of Lardo that the police had released to the media was perplexing, however. They claimed he was a person of interest. How had the police obtained such an accurate drawing of Lardo?

Tiny was adamant that no one had seen her and Lardo break into the home on Parkvale Street late one night. After they had silenced the homeowner for good and got rid of her body, Lardo had remained indoors as Jane had instructed. Tiny assured her that Lardo hadn't stepped outside until they had all driven off in the SUV that final night.

So how had the police discovered that Lardo was implicated in the kidnapping? Someone must have seen him.

The old lady next door. It had to be her. That nosy neighbor had gawked at them as they were leaving the house.

How long had she been standing in the rain with her dog, watching Lardo while he transported the bins to the SUV? Whether the old lady could see clearly from that distance was debatable, but who else would have been able to identify him so well?

Jane was still fuming about the open garage door. Curious

passersby would have questioned why a stocky stranger was loading bins in an unfamiliar vehicle parked in their elderly neighbor's garage. Who had decided to open the garage door anyway?

Was it Tiny? Lardo?

Yes, most people were expendable. Tiny would be the first to go. She'd served her purpose, but she'd made too many foolish mistakes. Although it would work to Jane's advantage, asking Ken to come to the cabin to deliver her drugs was Tiny's last blunder.

Jane was convinced that Lardo would relish his payback moment. It would be his chance to settle a score with Tiny.

And later, she'd get rid of him too.

31

MICHAEL

Saturday afternoon

Michael had no idea how much Darcy Barlow knew about his daughter's escape from jail. He would have to rely on his reporter's instincts to guide him during their conversation.

After Michael introduced himself, Mr. Barlow suggested they sit in a secluded corner of the visitors' room where they could chat without being interrupted. The man clearly wasn't enthusiastic about sharing his private life with too many people.

Mr. Barlow eased into an armchair and adjusted his wool cardigan. "If I hadn't had a stroke years ago, I'd be living on my own. My doctor told me I could have another one any day now because I have high blood pressure. Sometimes I forget things too—like when to take my meds. My memory isn't what it used to be." He shrugged, as if his deteriorating health was an inevitable part of life.

"They treat you well here?" Michael asked as a matter of politeness.

"They'd better. I've known some of the staff since they were kids." He laughed softly. "Everyone knows everyone else in Sainte-Adèle." His contentment faded in the next moment. "Let's drop the pretense. I know exactly who you are. You're the reporter who dated my daughter. You testified against her and helped put her in prison."

"That's right."

He eyed Michael. "If you came here to talk about Jane, I'm afraid I can't help you."

"So you know she escaped from jail."

"Yes, I saw the news report on TV, but I have no idea where she is." He looked down.

Michael's instincts kicked in. The man was lying. "There's a chance she's in the area. Has she called you lately?"

Mr. Barlow stared out the window at the grounds. "I haven't spoken to her since the day they convicted her for the murders. I don't expect to hear from her again."

More lies. "Why would you say that?"

"Why? Because people like Jane self-destruct." His brow furrowed as he looked back at Michael. "Why did you come here?"

"Jane kidnapped my girlfriend, Megan Scott."

Astonishment spread across the man's face, and he hastily said, "I don't know anything about that."

"She called me and threatened to kill Megan by tonight. I have to find her."

"Like I told you, I can't help you."

"Can't or won't?"

Mr. Barlow's demeanor grew somber. "Nothing surprises me about my daughter anymore. She was often up to no good, trying to weasel me and everyone else out of money. I can't blame her much. It's not easy growing up without a mother." He noticed Michael's stunned expression. "I guess Jane didn't tell you."

"No, she didn't."

"My wife was prone to fits of irrational behavior early in our marriage. Sometimes she'd disappear for days and leave me to take care of Jane by myself. We had no family here. I had to pay someone to watch over her when I was working."

Michael didn't know that either, but he said nothing.

Mr. Barlow went on. "My wife did me a favor when she up and left me for another married man. Jane was a young girl at the time. I raised her on my own. As the years passed, I began to see traits of my wife in Jane. I thought it was a female thing. You know, mood swings."

Michael nodded. He knew all about Jane's mood swings.

"Jane left home when she was eighteen and went to Toronto. After her studies, she got a job as a paralegal. I felt she had dodged the bullet and done something respectable with her life. Several years later, she was arrested and sent to jail." He shook his head. "She let me down again."

Michael wasn't sure what he meant by *again*. He put their discussion back on track. "That was in the past. Right now, I need to find Megan before Jane kills her."

"You're asking the wrong person."

"I think you know where Jane is hiding. Do you want Megan's blood on your hands?"

Mr. Barlow frowned, contemplating the matter. "I was hoping it wouldn't end this way." He sighed. "This is what happens when a child doesn't have a mother."

Like father, like daughter. Both blamed others for their own mistakes. "You were there," Michael said.

"It's not the same." The man's eyes reflected unease. "Jane's in big trouble. She's backed herself into a corner, and it won't end well. I know it won't."

Since Mr. Barlow didn't get up and leave the room, Michael sensed he had something else on his mind. He tried a different approach. "If I can find your daughter in time, I can stop her from doing anything impulsive."

But the elderly man digressed. "I've worked hard all my life.

I took jobs in construction like lots of people did here decades ago. With help from my friends, I built a two-story cabin on a piece of land I inherited when my father died. Land around here is quite valuable these days. Ski lodges are expanding. Winter is a profitable season because of the tourists."

"Why are you telling me this?"

Mr. Barlow raised a forefinger. "Hear me out. Weeks before Jane left for Toronto, she asked me to sign over ownership of my property to her. The deal was that she'd allow me to continue living there, but I had to pay her rent. I thought she was joking. It was *my* property, but I had to pay her to live there? Give me a break."

"What did you do?"

"I refused to discuss it further. I told her the only way she'd get the land was over my dead body. I didn't think she'd take me seriously."

Michael leaned forward. "What do you mean?"

"I was driving down a winding road to town one day when the brakes on my truck malfunctioned. I steered right to avoid an oncoming car and crashed into a tree. I broke my leg and walk with a limp ever since. After the accident, a mechanic inspected my truck for insurance purposes. He asked me if I'd tampered with the brakes. I was flabbergasted." His eyes misted up. "How could someone do that to their own father?"

"Did you confront Jane about it?"

"I'll get to that part later." Mr. Barlow drew a deep breath. "As you can see, it still bothers me to this day. Anyway, because of the situation with the brakes, I couldn't claim insurance coverage. It would raise questions that I didn't want to answer. I paid the auto repairs and medical fees out of my own pocket."

Michael was astounded that Mr. Barlow had covered up for his daughter and wanted to protect her, despite her malicious plot to do him in. He tried not to judge the man. Jane had deceived and manipulated many people—even him.

Mr. Barlow continued. "At that point, I decided I'd done

everything I could for Jane. I got her out of tough situations and received nothing in return. It was always take, take, take." He blinked, as if to erase those memories. "After I got back on my feet, I kicked her out."

"So she didn't leave on her own," Michael said.

"The money I gave her helped push her out the door. She knew she couldn't make a life for herself in a small town and had wanted to live in a big city anyway. The move was a step in the right direction for her. And for me. I've forgiven her since then. It wasn't her fault she grew up like that. Now she's back in my life. *Our* lives." His lips tightened.

"Does Jane have access to your cabin?"

"I wouldn't know."

"She might have taken Megan there. Where's the cabin?"

"I don't remember."

Michael refrained from mentioning he'd met Henri in town and found out approximately where the cabin was located. He didn't want to cause trouble between two old friends. "Why are you covering up for Jane?"

The old man's lips quivered.

Michael understood. "You're scared. You believe she'll come after you next if you talk."

Mr. Barlow remained silent.

"I'm calling the police as soon as I leave here. We'll knock on every door in the area if we have to."

Mr. Barlow's eyes narrowed. "Jane is as slippery as a snake and as vicious."

"I can take care of myself."

"Are you carrying?"

"What?"

Mr. Barlow edged slightly forward. "Jane knows how to use a gun. She's an excellent shot."

"So?"

"I took her hunting in her teenage years. Taught her a few

things about nature and self-preservation. You should know..." He hesitated. "There's a shotgun in the cabin."

"Where's the cabin?" Michael asked again.

Mr. Barlow's shoulders sagged. "The police will find her. I know they will."

Michael couldn't tell if he was referring to Jane or Megan. Replying in equally vague terms, he said, "It would be better if I found her first. Tell me how to get to your cabin."

Without saying another word, Mr. Barlow stood up and grabbed his cane. He nodded at the attendant who strode over. "Take me back to my room."

It was raining again. Michael got into his car and watched the raindrops slide down the windshield as he mentally reviewed his conversation with Mr. Barlow.

Although Jane's father was disturbed by the way his daughter had turned out, he continued to protect her. He had lied about not remembering where the cabin was located and maybe about recent contacts with Jane too. She was a fugitive, and he was harboring her.

Michael had noticed the man's apprehension. The way he cut short their meeting and hurried out. Fear paralyzes people, keeps them from talking. Mr. Barlow believed that Jane would go after him and finish him off if he talked. The guy was afraid of his own daughter.

Michael reached for his phone and called Esposito.

After he briefed the detective on his findings, Esposito said, "Sit tight. I'll get in touch with the Quebec Provincial Police and ask them to locate the cabin. I'll keep you in the loop."

Michael thanked him and hung up, but he couldn't wait for Esposito or the QPP to get back to him. He had to find that cabin and fast.

One thing was inevitable: If he succeeded in finding Jane, it would lead to a tragic confrontation between them. And it wouldn't only be a battle of wits. He might have to kill Jane to save Megan—and save himself. With Jane as the mastermind behind Megan's disappearance, he was about to encounter his worst challenge yet.

Was he up to taking the biggest risk of his life?

He accessed his parents' home number. He needed to hear a familiar voice. Since he had no idea what lay ahead, he had to face the truth. It might be the last time he'd speak with them.

But no one answered.

He left a message.

Maybe it was for the better. He had to think straight and keep his feelings under control. His top priority was finding Megan. More than ever, he had to trust that he would get to her in time.

He had an hour or two at the most to locate Darcy Barlow's cabin before sunset. He retrieved his laptop and accessed the satellite image of the area. Henri had told him Darcy Barlow's cabin was situated across the lake from Hôtel Le Chantecler. It had an L-shaped wharf that jutted out from the property.

Michael had spent weekends with his friends in the lake area a decade earlier and was familiar with it. What he didn't expect to see on the satellite image was the eruption of cabins that had sprung up since then.

Almost each property had a wharf. Three properties had the same L-shaped docks and shared a patch of shoreline. His mission had now become all the more complicated.

He veered onto Morin Road and followed it along the edge of the lake. He'd have to park a safe distance from the cabins and approach them without being seen. Jane probably had the big guy keeping watch in case anyone set foot on the property.

A glance at his rearview mirror indicated that a blue sedan was tailing him. Was it the same one he'd seen earlier?

The guy was following him too close. Michael sped up, trying to put distance between them.

The blue sedan increased its speed.

The hair rose on Michael's arms. It had to be the same sedan!

Was it Gabe Rivard?

There was a curve ahead. The road was slick from the rainfall. He had to maneuver it carefully or he'd land in a ditch. He touched the brake pedal as a warning to the guy shadowing him to slow down.

It had the reverse effect.

The sedan sped up and rammed into him.

Michael jerked forward and fought to control his car. That lunatic was trying to drive him off the road!

The sedan rammed into him again.

Michael kept a firm grasp on the steering wheel and tried to maneuver the car, but it skidded off the road. His stomach lurched as the ground fell away beneath him.

The car hurtled through the air.

Shrubbery ahead of him.

Crunching sounds.

The car landed with a thud and teetered on its side just as the airbag blew up in his face.

Then darkness.

32

—————

MEGAN

Saturday night

My lips were dry, and I was so thirsty.

When was the last time I'd had a drink of water, let alone eaten something?

Not knowing whether it was day or night made me feel as if I were floating in a void where time had been suspended, where there was no past or future, only the vast blackness of now.

I propped myself against a wall. I pushed my back against the hardness to establish that it was real and not something I was imagining.

It was dark, and the piercing music and strobe lights had stopped again. All I could hear was the ringing in my ears.

The door suddenly opened a crack. Was I imagining it?

A loud creak on the steps meant someone was retreating upstairs. Had I imagined that too? No. Wooden floorboards in rustic cabins were known to creak.

I reached out and touched the door with my manacled hands. It gave way!

I pushed harder and it swung open.

I could barely make out the living room furniture. It wasn't from my lack of ability to see properly but rather from the dimness enveloping the cabin.

It was nighttime. Which day of the week it was, I wouldn't know.

I tried to get up, but my legs felt numb. I crawled out of the closet on my hands and knees and looked around. I was alone.

Moonlight cast an eerie light over the kitchen table and chairs thirty feet ahead of me. A cool breeze reached me. I peered through the darkness. Someone had left the cabin door open. I could see the screen door leading outside.

Had Tiny or Lardo inadvertently provided me with an opportunity to escape? Had one of them conveniently set up the other to take the blame if I did?

Or was this ruse part of the deadly game Jane was playing with me? Was I a convenient target that she wanted to toy with in the middle of the night?

A small bottle of water glistened on the kitchen table. My mouth salivated as I imagined the sensation of cool water over my tongue. Was it real?

I had to find out.

Unsure if I'd be able to stand up without any support, I crawled to an armchair and pushed myself up. The floor was cold. They'd taken away my socks and shoes. I didn't care. I felt liberated.

My legs were wobbly, but I could walk. I made it to the table and grabbed the bottle of water. It was half full but was the best thing I had ever tasted. I drank it all in seconds flat.

I needed to find a flashlight. I'd seen Jane use one the night we arrived. I slowly pulled open the drawers under the kitchen counter, careful not to make any noise. I looked inside each one. The flashlight had to be in one of them.

The third drawer ended my search. I grabbed the flashlight and flicked it on. The batteries were functional.

A floorboard creaked.

I swung around and took a step backward, almost losing my balance.

No one.

I could have imagined it, but if someone were playing a trick on me, I wasn't going to hang around to find out. I had to get out. Now!

I moved toward the screen door and gently opened it. I flinched as it squeaked. I listened. Nothing. The sound hadn't been loud enough to alert the others.

Using the rail for support, I descended the wooden steps. The uneven ground was covered with large pieces of gravel, making it painful to walk in bare feet.

I paused for a moment and inhaled deeply. The cool night air carried the scent of damp earth and foliage and the promise of freedom. I looked around to get my bearings and determine the best route of escape. Thick trees against the backdrop of night blocked my view on all sides except for an opening before me that led to the lake.

But the lake wasn't an option unless there was a boat nearby, and I couldn't see one from where I stood. The shoreline was obscure and could be farther away than I anticipated. I couldn't risk walking over there from this point either. I'd be in the open and someone might see me from the cabin.

Over my shoulder was the SUV. Maybe Jane had left the keys inside and I could drive away.

I circled the SUV and tried to open each door. They were locked.

My attention shifted to the gravel path that twisted back up to the main road. I could chance it, but I didn't want to risk running off like a crazy woman into an unfamiliar landscape at night. The darkness could be so deadly. With bears and other wildlife in the area, I might meet a worse fate than the one Jane planned for me.

I felt lightheaded, as if I were floating in a dream state. Was I imagining all this?

I bent over and picked up some leaves. I crushed them in my hand. They felt real enough.

A cold gust of wind hit me, and I shivered. My short-sleeved shirt exposed bare arms. Where was my jacket? Inside the cabin?

No, I couldn't go back there. They would lock me in the closet again, and small spaces weren't safe. I had to leave this horrid place. I had to make it happen right now.

To begin with, I had to hide.

If Michael were with me, which path would he choose?

I darted into the woodland about twenty feet to my left, hoping the shadows would keep me invisible. I caught a glimpse through the rows of trees that separated me from the shore.

Ribbons of moonlight danced on the surface of the water. Maybe the lake wasn't such a bad choice after all. I might even be able to swim across it. Using the flashlight to guide me, I made my way there.

Stones. Splinters of wood. Jagged soil. They cut into my bare feet, slowing me down, while tree branches scratched my arms and face. It didn't matter. I had to keep going.

I shuffled through a patch of leaves and tripped over a tree root, landing on my chin and twisting my ankle. The flashlight flew from my hand. Sharp pain shot through my kneecaps. I put a hand over my mouth to silence my screams.

No! Don't stop!

I leaned against a tree trunk and forced myself up. My ankle throbbed with pain. I hobbled over to retrieve the flashlight. I had to reach the shore. It was my sole chance for survival.

The trees grew sparser now. I felt softness underfoot as the path opened up before me. The beam from the flashlight confirmed I had reached a sandy beach. It felt so much better under my feet than stones and wood. I advanced several more yards and stopped.

I aimed the beam farther along the shore to my right. There was a dock, but I couldn't see a boat.

I directed the light at the surface of the water.

Oh, no! I'd underestimated the size of the lake. I couldn't possibly swim across it, not with my hands bound and my ankle in so much pain.

Tears flowed down my cheeks. There had to be a way out.

What would Michael do?

The flashlight!

I sat down and aimed it toward the opposite shore. Michael had taught me how to use a signal mirror when we'd gone hiking once. A flashlight might be as effective. I prayed like I'd never prayed before that someone—anyone—would see my SOS signal.

Three long flashes followed by three shorter ones. Repeat.

I stared into the blackness across the lake, anticipating some kind of response. Nothing. Even though my hand ached, I kept the pace going and continued to send out my emergency beacon.

Three long flashes. Three shorter ones.

Repeat.

Repeat.

Repeat.

Noises behind me.

I wasn't fast enough.

Someone grabbed me by the hair and yanked me upward, jerking the flashlight out of my grasp.

"You pitiful excuse for a woman!" Jane slapped me hard across the face.

I lost my balance and fell to the ground.

"Do you think for one second that someone will come and rescue you?" She laughed. "I'll break you long before then."

I tasted blood. My head was spinning, but I kept my eyes on Jane.

She shook her fist in my face. "I swear, I'm this close to bashing your head in!"

I flinched, waiting for another blow.

She took hold of my hair again and pulled me to my feet. "Get inside, you cheating tramp!"

A sense of survival surged inside me, followed by a burst of anger. I swung my arms and hit Jane hard, my handcuffs striking her right cheek.

She screamed and released her hold on me. She put a hand to her face. "You'll regret this! Trust me."

Lardo stole out of the shadows in the next instant and grabbed my arm.

"Take her inside and lock her up in the closet," Jane said to him. "Then go gather more wood for the fireplace. I'll deal with you and Tiny later."

"But boss, I didn't do nothin'," Lardo said.

"Go!" Jane shouted.

Lardo dragged me toward the cabin, the muscles in my legs depleted.

I couldn't imagine what escalated punishment Jane had in store for me. Would it be my execution?

I didn't want to die.

But if this was the end of the road for me, at least I'd shown her that I was a force to be reckoned with.

33

MICHAEL

Saturday night

The beam from a flashlight blinded Michael. He raised a hand to block it.

"Are you okay, sir?" a male voice asked.

The beam shifted to the front of the car, revealing that the vehicle was tilted to the right.

Michael perceived the cracked windshield and the tree branches covering it. He remembered how he'd tried to steer the car before it skidded off the road. Other than a stiffness in his neck, he felt no pain elsewhere. No broken bones and no blood, despite the crash.

"Yes, I'm okay."

The man opened the driver's door and offered him a hand. "You are very lucky." He spoke with a French-Canadian accent. "Ten more feet to the left and you would have ended up like the other guy. I called the police. They will be here soon. My name is Paul Lapointe, by the way."

"Thank you, Paul." Michael introduced himself, then surveyed the crash site from the road.

To the left of the shallow ditch where his car had come to an abrupt stop, the landscape dipped thirty feet into a ravine. The blue sedan that had forced him off the road was at the bottom, nose first, its taillights lit up.

"Any sign of life down there?" Michael asked Paul.

"I heard no calls for help. The driver could be unconscious —or worse."

"You saw what happened?"

"I sure did. The driver was trying to run you off the road. What a fool."

A QPP officer arrived minutes later. Officer Leblanc radioed his detachment and asked that first responders be sent to the scene, as well as a tow truck. From what Michael overheard, it would take twenty minutes for the ambulance, firefighters, and tow truck to arrive from Sainte-Agathe, a neighboring town.

The officer inspected Michael's driver's license and took notes as he described the incident. After he went through the same routine with Paul, a local resident, the officer told him he was free to leave.

Officer Leblanc's radio crackled with an incoming call. His earlier request for a verification of the license plate on the blue sedan confirmed that the car had been stolen.

Michael suspected that Gabe Rivard had been behind the wheel. Maybe the ex-con had come to town to connect with members of the illegal drug operation that Willie had told him about. It's possible that Rivard got sidetracked when he spotted him. Or maybe he'd followed Michael from Montreal and seized the opportunity to try to get rid of him.

In any case, the cops wouldn't be able to verify the driver's identity until they'd rescued him from the ravine. Michael would have to hang around until then.

Officer Leblanc turned to him. "What brings you here to Sainte-Adèle?"

"I'm an investigative reporter. I'm working on a missing person case with the Montreal police."

"What case is that?"

He recapped the details, including Esposito's imminent call to local law enforcement for their assistance in finding Megan. "Can you radio your detachment to find out if the detective contacted them?"

Officer Leblanc obliged.

The answer came back in the negative.

Michael had one last request. "Officer, I'm looking for Darcy Barlow's cabin. Megan might be held there against her will."

"I don't know anyone by the name Barlow," the officer said. "I was going to suggest you try the Registry, but they're closed for the weekend."

Old news. However, Esposito might have more influence in digging up that information once he reached local authorities.

Another call came through the officer's radio. He responded to the dispatcher's request to verify suspicious flashing lights along the shoreline bordering Morin Road. "I can be there in an hour," he said into his shoulder microphone, then received confirmation.

"Busy night for a small town," Michael said to him. "Flashing lights?"

"Teens come up here on weekends and like to play pranks," Officer Leblanc said with a twinkle in his eye. "It's routine to investigate such incidents."

Weekend pranks. Some things never changed. "Is there a place in town where I can rent a car?"

"No, you'll have to go to Sainte-Agathe for that. Twenty minutes away."

Michael checked his watch. The minutes he would spend elsewhere would eat away at the precious time remaining— time better spent searching for Megan.

His thoughts drifted back to Esposito. Why hadn't he called the QPP yet? Or even him?

He put in a call to the detective, but it went to his voicemail. He didn't bother leaving a message.

The first responders finally arrived and set up an emergency lighting system. After they had extracted the driver from the car and hoisted him out of the ravine, they told Officer Leblanc that the man had a broken leg and a head injury. They would have to transport him to the hospital in the next town.

Michael observed the unconscious man on the gurney. Despite the blood spatter on his face, he recognized him. It was Gabe Rivard.

He approached Officer Leblanc. "I know this man." He briefed him on Rivard's recent shooting attempt in Montreal and emphasized the ex-con's connection to the Hells Angels.

An ensuing verification of Rivard's papers confirmed his identity. Officer Leblanc radioed the detachment and relayed the details. He requested another police cruiser ASAP to escort the ambulance to the hospital.

After the tow truck had hauled Michael's car to a local garage, he asked the owner if he could rent one of the used cars he had on the lot. The owner claimed it wasn't his standard practice to rent out cars.

Michael was having none of it. He pulled out his wallet. The garage owner conceded that his generous cash payout was more than enough to cover expenses for the weekend.

Retracing his journey, Michael set out along Morin Road in his rental car. He was no further ahead in finding Megan. With time running out and the night swallowing him up, he had to rely on his instincts to guide him now more than ever.

According to the satellite image he'd viewed, spidery roads ran downhill from Morin Road to each of the three cabins with an L-shaped wharf. Megan was in one of them. He felt it in his gut.

He drove down the first road and reduced his speed as he passed a cabin. He rolled down the passenger window.

Sounds of people laughing and soft music reached him. Three cars were parked outside. He reached for his binoculars in his backpack and spotted a group of people, young and old, sitting indoors by a fireplace. Signs that he could move on. He returned the binoculars to his backpack.

He repeated the routine for the next road that meandered downhill. This time, he came across two cabins. There were no sounds from either one. No vehicles were parked on either property. The cabins appeared to have been shut down for the season. He drove off to the next destination.

The third road off Morin Road wound downward and cut through a dense stretch of forest. He came to a stop at a fork in the road. Great. Now what?

Michael turned right, then turned left at the next split. He could backtrack if he discovered he'd made a mistake.

He would have driven past the cabin had he not spotted something moving between the trees. A deer? A human?

Turning off the headlights, he veered onto a secondary path and parked. He reached for his backpack containing two bottles of water, the binoculars, a first-aid kit, and a hunting knife. The latter was an afterthought. He didn't know what he'd find, but if this cabin belonged to Darcy Barlow, the people inside it were a lot more dangerous—and more equipped—than he was.

Michael advanced cautiously toward the area in the forest where he'd seen movement. Careful not to alert anyone to his presence, he kept his flashlight aimed at the ground. The trees soon thinned out to the left of him and he could see part of a lake.

Voices drifted his way. He could tell that they originated from somewhere up ahead and farther to the right, rather than from the shore.

He turned off his flashlight and took out his binoculars. A chimney spewed smoke about thirty feet ahead.

He crept closer. A cabin came into view, its front door facing the shoreline.

He zigzagged through the trees until he saw a partially open window on one side of the cabin. He lifted his binoculars and zoomed in to get a better view.

He froze.

He recognized her even from a distance.

Jane Barlow!

A gentle glow flickered inside the cabin from a fireplace or lantern. Jane was gesturing and shouting something he couldn't make out.

A dark-haired man stood next to her. He was a live version of Enrico's sketch. The tall and massive guy also fit Dorothy's description of the male passenger she'd seen in her neighbor's garage.

Michael's phone vibrated. He fumbled for it in his jacket and almost dropped it. He answered.

It was Esposito. "Michael, we found a thumbprint matching Megan's in the Parkvale Street house. Her initials were engraved in the cement floor in the basement too."

Megan had found a way to let him know she'd been there after all. Smart cookie.

"Michael? Are you there?"

"Yes," he whispered.

"We also got a lead on that sketch of the big man you sent me. A witness identified him as one of the occupants of an SUV in Sainte-Adèle a couple of nights ago. He was changing a tire on a road by the lake. Two women were helping him. One tall, the other short."

"And Megan?"

"The witness claimed he saw another woman inside the car, but he couldn't see her too well. It was dark and drizzling."

"It means Megan might still be alive," Michael whispered.

"You'll have to speak up," Esposito said. "I'm on the highway, and I have a hard time hearing you." The sound of windshield wipers broke the silence.

"Go on," Michael said, louder this time.

"I left the best for last. Ken Reilly came in to see me. He received a call from Tanya Cordi—or rather, Tiny—requesting a delivery of drugs. We're on our way there right now."

"To the lakeside cabin in Sainte-Adèle?"

"Yes. How did you know?"

"Because I'm hiding in the woods outside the place. I can see Jane Barlow and a guy the size of a gorilla inside."

Esposito swore. "Stay put until we get there. It won't take us more than half an hour." When Michael didn't answer, the detective shouted, "You hear me? Don't do anything until we arrive."

"It might be too late by then." Michael ended the call.

34

———

MEGAN

Saturday night

Exhaustion had set in, but I couldn't sleep.

I'd become a conduit for the strobe lights and shrieking music running through my body, mind, and soul. A persistent migraine and hunger pains would finish me off if Jane didn't.

Massive gray blobs had formed in the closet. They floated around me ever so softly, then suffocated me until I coughed so hard, I spit blood. I tried to disperse them, but they kept attacking me as if they had a mind of their own.

My sanity. Something I was losing steadily as the hours went by. Or had it been days? My judgment was so fuzzy that I wasn't sure about anything anymore.

My throat was parched. My lips were cracked and sore. I needed water.

Jane had given me a sip of water earlier, but it tasted weird, like the other times. I drank it anyway. I hadn't eaten since—I didn't know when—and yet I felt queasy. My stomach was empty, so I didn't have to worry about vomiting.

I wasn't quite dead but would soon be. Would I survive until tomorrow? Or even the next hour? Soon Jane would claim victory and tell Michael she'd succeeded in turning me into a corpse.

I couldn't let her win. I refused to let her win. I had to fight her with every ounce of energy left inside me. I had to imagine good thoughts to counteract the bad ones stuck inside Jane's head. Good prevailed over bad. It was a universal principle.

So was survival of the fittest.

Except that I wasn't the fittest. Far from it. Soon my heart would stop beating, my mind would go blank, and I would no longer exist.

Michael had often told me I had a strong mind. Together we had defeated Jane when she tried to deceive us. Together we could do it again. Although exhaustion was consuming me, I forced myself to imagine Michael rushing to my rescue and reaching my side. He might even be riding one of those gray blobs right now, getting closer and closer to me.

The screeching music and flashing lights stopped. The only thing that persisted was the ringing in my ears.

No, wait. There was another sound, like the rush of the ocean one hears in a seashell. The piercing music had left its imprint on my brain. How sad. My brain has turned into a large seashell. I could envision it now, riding away on one of those gray blobs.

A faint shaft of light filtered into the closet as the door slowly opened. Someone was standing there. I squinted to see who it was.

Tiny. She handed me a bottle of water. I grabbed it and drank, disappointed to find that it contained only a few drops.

She snatched it from me and turned away, hiding the bottle behind her back. With her free hand, she pushed the door shut but didn't succeed in closing it completely. It sprang open.

"I don't know what you're talking about," Tiny shouted. "I came downstairs for some water."

"Do you take me for an idiot?" another woman yelled, her tone spiteful. "Come with me, you little liar."

I recognized the voice. It was the bad Jane. The cruel and angry Jane.

I pressed on the door to open it a crack so I could see what was happening. If this was real and not an illusion, I had to pay attention.

A soft glow from the fireplace flickered over Tiny's pajamas as she hesitantly followed Jane into the kitchen. Lardo was there too. A lantern sat on the table, sending eerie shadows up the walls. Standing before them, Tiny looked like a child.

Jane placed her hands on her hips. She was wearing a sweater and jeans. Lardo was in jeans too. Why weren't they in pajamas like Tiny?

Overnight bags sat by the door. Were they getting ready to go somewhere?

Jane's face contorted with anger. She screamed at Tiny and waved her hands in the air. I couldn't hear what she was saying because my ears were buzzing. As Jane hovered closer to the lantern, I noticed a bandage on her right cheek. How did she get hurt? When had that happened?

I needed to hear what they were saying. I swallowed and my ears popped. I managed to hear a bit better, but the words were muffled.

Lardo stood by, his arms folded, watching the two women. His silly grin implied he was enjoying their back-and-forth squabble.

Jane turned to him and said something.

Lardo shook his head no.

Jane glared at Tiny with explosive anger. She lunged at her and pushed her hard.

Tiny shrieked and fell on her back, her bottle of water spinning across the floor.

I watched in horror as Jane kicked Tiny in the ribs. Once. Twice. She pointed at Lardo and shouted something.

He gripped Tiny's arms and lifted her up, her legs dangling in the air. He laughed, holding her higher and higher while she screeched and squirmed. He kept on laughing until Jane raised her hand and said something to him. Confused, he stopped.

In the next instant, Lardo nodded and set Tiny down. While she tried to steady herself by placing a hand on a chair, he punched her in the head. He caught her as she went limp.

Oh, my God! Was she dead?

He placed Tiny on the floor where she remained motionless. He mumbled something that I couldn't make out.

Jane opened the kitchen drawers, one by one, frantically searching. She handed Lardo some rope.

He bound Tiny's hands and feet, then lifted her in his arms, her unconscious body floppy like that of a rag doll. He hurried out, rushed down the steps, and vanished into the blackness.

Jane stood in the doorway. She shouted and waved at him with both hands, as if she were instructing him to go far, far away.

Terror swept over me. Was I next?

I jerked away from the door, not wanting to accept what I'd just witnessed. No. This can't be happening. I felt as if I were going to pass out. I breathed in deeply, willing my heart to slow down.

I peeked through the narrow opening in the door. The cabin was dark. Nobody was around. Had I imagined the whole thing?

The door slammed shut in my face.

No!

Music blasted and lights flashed.

I curled up on the floor. The gray blobs were approaching, getting larger and larger, encircling me.

I welcomed them and prayed the end would come soon.

35

MICHAEL

Saturday night

It was almost midnight.

Michael crouched behind a tree trunk, keeping an eye on the open window at the side of the cabin. Jane's loud and livid words carried through the stillness of the night.

"Lardo, it's your turn to make it right, so do it," Jane shouted at the massive guy, urging him into action.

Lardo. So that was his name.

Michael couldn't see the guy anymore, but he heard him moving around and laughing loudly. A woman was screaming, over and over.

Was it Megan? What the hell was going on in there?

Jane raised a hand. "Get rid of her! Now!"

More movement. The screaming stopped.

Michael's breath stuck in his throat.

"She's not moving," Lardo said, sounding both surprised and satisfied. "She was mean to me. She said bad things about me. I did what you told me, boss. I killed her."

Adrenaline surged through Michael's body. Were they talking about Megan?

All of a sudden, Jane charged to the left and dropped out of his line of sight. The sound of drawers opening and closing. A flurry of activity. What was she looking for?

She reappeared in the window and handed Lardo some rope. "Tie her up and take her outside."

Michael darted to the corner of the cabin and hid behind thick bushes where he had a partial view of the front steps. He had to know if it was Megan.

Lardo panted down the steps and hurried to the beach, his wide back blocking Michael's view of the woman in his arms.

"Paddle to the middle of the lake and throw her in!" Jane's words spewed from the doorway.

Michael's heart pounded faster. He had to stop Lardo before he dumped Megan in the lake.

He was about to leap out from behind the bushes but stopped. As Lardo repositioned his cargo over his left shoulder, moonlight reflected off the woman's blonde hair and her small frame.

It wasn't Megan in Lardo's arms after all. It was Tiny!

Lardo transported Tiny to the quay. He headed to the right of the wharf and placed her body in a canoe. Until now, Michael hadn't noticed the canoe docked in the shadows.

He watched as Lardo paddled to the middle of the lake and vanished in the darkness. Minutes later, a splash confirmed that he'd thrown Tiny's body overboard.

With the big guy in the middle of the lake, Michael saw his chance to save Megan. He checked around the corner. Jane had gone back inside the cabin. If he had to, he could overpower her. He couldn't wait for the cops to arrive. He had to make a move now.

He scuttled out of his hiding place. He could barely decipher Lardo paddling back to shore. He didn't have much time.

Inhaling sharply, he raced up the steps.

He crept into the unlit kitchen and snuck toward the back of the floor, which was equally in darkness. Jane wasn't around. Maybe she'd gone upstairs.

Was Megan there too?

He listened, heard the creaking of floorboards upstairs. Climbing the flight of stairs would mean a confrontation with Jane. He wanted to avoid that.

But maybe Megan wasn't upstairs. Maybe she was in the basement.

No. Cottages in small towns didn't typically have basements.

The door by the stairs drew his attention. Was it a closet? What if Darcy Barlow's shotgun was in there? Better yet, what if the gun were loaded? A definite advantage for him.

As he neared, he noticed the door had a bolt lock on it. He put a hand on the closet door and felt a low vibration. Strange. He slid open the lock and opened the door. Blasting music and flashing lights almost threw him off his feet.

Megan!

Relief, then shock, flooded over him as he perceived her, curled up in a corner of the closet. Her knees were bent, her hands in shackles. She was gazing into a void, as if she'd drifted into a catatonic state.

Michael fumbled for a switch along the outer wall, not certain if any of them would stop the strobe lights from flashing or the shrill music from piercing his eardrums. He flicked all of them and it worked, with the added benefit of a fixture in the ceiling lighting up this part of the cabin.

He bent over Megan and put a hand on her shoulder. "Megan, can you hear me? It's Michael. I'm going to take you to a safe place now."

She turned her head in his direction. Her face was pale and gaunt. What bothered him the most was her glazed expression. Her eyes showed no sign of recognition.

What had Jane done to her?

Footsteps hastened down the stairs.

He swirled around.

Jane!

She hadn't changed much in the last five years. She was still captivating in the same unnerving way, like a cougar preparing to pounce on its prey.

He stood in the doorway, blocking her path, determined not to let her get any closer to Megan.

"Michael, I knew you'd find me." Jane's gaze flitted over him, undressing him, violating him. She smiled. "It's terrific to see you again."

He clenched his jaw. "What have you done to Megan?"

Jane glimpsed the open closet. "Close the door. You don't have to bother with her anymore. She's finished."

Michael didn't budge.

She moved up to him, wrapped her arms around his neck. "It's been a while, but I intend to make up for lost time."

He clasped her arms and shoved her away. "Go to hell!"

She stumbled backwards but steadied herself.

Michael turned away and lifted Megan in his arms. He was astonished at how much weight she'd lost.

"This is a chance for a fresh start for us, Michael," Jane said, standing in his way. "We can go anywhere you want. I promise I'll make you the happiest man in the world."

"I wouldn't want to be with you if you were the last woman on earth." He pushed past her.

"Hey, you!" a male voice boomed from the doorway. Lardo charged toward him like a raging bull.

Michael barely had time to place Megan on the floor.

Lardo swooped down on him faster than he could have predicted. With mammoth hands, he clutched Michael's arms and dragged him across the kitchen floor.

Michael fought to break his hold, but he was no match for Lardo's gargantuan grip.

"Lardo, stop!" Jane's tone was sharp. "Let go of him. He's my man." She pointed a shotgun at him.

Lardo released his hold on Michael. "Your man?"

"That's right, you greasy chunk of fat," she shouted. "Get the hell out of here!"

"But—but—I was tryin' to help you, boss." Lardo took a step toward her.

Jane tightened her grip on the shotgun. "I don't need your help anymore. You heard me. Get out!"

Michael rose from the floor. His arms ached from the force of Lardo's grasp, but it was a minor problem compared to what was unfolding now. Jane's intentions were serious—and deadly. He slowly moved out of the gun's direct path.

"But—but I did what you wanted, boss. I didn't make no mistakes." Lardo shook his head. "Not like Tiny."

"I don't give a damn." Jane reduced the space between them. "You're history."

Michael detected movement beyond Jane. Megan was crawling on the floor and trying to get to the armchair in the living room. Probably to hide.

He needed to distract Jane. "Don't do this, Jane," he pleaded. "Let him go. What purpose would it serve to kill him?"

"Please don't tell me what to do, Michael." Jane drew closer, adjusting her aim at Lardo.

Lardo turned and flew out the door. He scrambled down the steps to the sandy patch, but he wasn't fast enough.

Jane fired a shot. Then another.

Lardo fell to the ground, his horizontal body protruding like a dark mound against the backdrop of the shimmering lake.

36

MEGAN

Saturday night

Michael said he was taking me to a safe place. At least, I thought he did. Maybe he hadn't been here at all. His touch had been so comforting, though.

The relentless music had stopped. The flashing lights were gone. I was stretched out on the cabin floor and gazing at an antique Tiffany pendant light in the ceiling. Such vivid colors!

Mumbled voices drifted from the kitchen. The humming in my ears prevented me from hearing the words clearly. I turned my head to see who was talking.

Jane was pointing a shotgun at Lardo.

Was I hallucinating again?

I blinked hard.

It was true. Michael was in the kitchen too.

I tried to stand, but cramps contracted the muscles in my legs. I almost yelled out in pain, but I suppressed it. I couldn't show Jane that I'd escaped. Especially not the bad Jane who was now holding a shotgun.

I remembered how I'd slithered away from the closet like a

worm escaping the pull of an abyss, dragging myself along the floor, inch by inch. I had to get out of Jane's line of sight now in case she turned around and saw me.

I squirmed my way to the nearest armchair and hid behind it. Using the armrest for support, I pulled myself up so that I could perch on my knees and peek into the kitchen.

Lardo muttered something and shook his head at Jane. He tugged on his T-shirt. I'd never seen him look so scared.

Michael extended his arms toward Jane as if he were trying to persuade her to put down the gun. Maybe he'd seen me and was trying to distract her.

Lardo took a few steps back, then swiftly turned and ran out the door.

Jane fired a shot!

Lardo's arms flailed. She shot him again, and he tumbled in a heap on the ground.

I trembled, took in rapid breaths. Would I be next?

Jane lowered her gun but kept a tight hold on it. Her stony manner chilled me, and I feared for Michael's safety.

But they remained in the kitchen, talking.

I strained to hear what they were saying. If only the noise in my ears would stop...

All of a sudden, Jane shouted, "Admit it, Michael. You couldn't stay away from me. That's why you came here, isn't it? If you truly love me, you have to say the words. Say you love me. Say it!"

He calmly said, "I can't."

She shrilled, "After all these years, you're still hooked on that poor excuse for a woman. Can't you see she wasn't right for you? You only stayed with her because you felt pity for her. You felt responsible for her husband's death."

"You're wrong." He raised his voice. "None of that is true."

"She's useless to you. She's just a vegetable. Or haven't you noticed?"

"Can't you play fair and do the right thing for once?"

Jane laughed. "That's exactly what I'm doing. I'm playing fair with you. I'm giving you a second chance."

"A second chance? For what?"

"It's simple. I'm giving you the opportunity to make up for your past mistake by choosing me over her this time."

Michael glared at her. "*My* past mistake? What about *your* past mistake? Like when you hired someone to kill Megan's husband."

"It was an accident. A case of mistaken identity."

"Right. How could I forget? Megan and I were your original targets. From what I can see, old habits die hard."

Jane raised her chin. "That's not true. Some things have changed. You're here now. With me. It's the right choice for both of us."

"Come on. You know how the legal system works. Draw on your sense of justice and give yourself up."

"And spend the rest of my days in jail? What fun is that? We can walk out of here and have a fantastic new life together."

He grinned. "What makes you think I'd leave here with a woman holding a shotgun?"

"You have to trust me, Michael. I would never do anything to hurt you."

"Trust is earned, never given."

"I can give you a lot more than trust."

"You need professional help, Jane."

"Been there, done it. And you know what? I beat them at their own mind games." She snickered. "What makes me happy is that you and I can finally be together. I've waited for this moment for so long. Don't ruin it for me, Michael."

"How far do you think you'll get? You've already knocked off two people here."

"I'm a shrewd businesswoman." Her tone grew curt. "I hire people, then get rid of them. They're expendable for different reasons. So is Megan."

I cringed.

Michael held out his hand. "Give me the gun. This isn't how you want things to end."

He kept talking to Jane, buying time. Yet I couldn't imagine how we'd leave here alive.

At the least, I wouldn't.

Michael went on. "The cops are onto you. It won't be long before they arrive and surround the place."

"Ha!" Jane scoffed. "Good try. No one knows where I am. By the time they find this cabin, you and I will be long gone."

"You're wrong on both counts. I'm not leaving Megan. You're on your own."

Still pointing her shotgun at him, Jane glanced over her shoulder. She noticed the open closet and dashed toward it.

Oh, no! I ducked and squeezed into a ball, hoping she wouldn't see me.

Jane peered inside the closet, then turned around. She spotted me squatting by the armchair. She raised her gun and aimed it at me.

"No!" I tried to crawl further away, toward Michael, but she followed me, keeping her aim on me.

"Jane, don't shoot her!" he called out.

"I'll kill her! If you don't leave with me now, Michael, I swear I will."

"Okay, okay." He slowly advanced toward her, his hands held up. "I'll go with you. I promise."

"You're saying the words, but you don't really mean them. I know your technique. You're trying to trick me."

He stopped, his eyes alert. It was as if he were trying to come up with a reason to regain her trust in him, or else she would kill both of us.

"Well?" She prompted him. "Show me you mean it."

"Okay. On the drive here, I leased a used car. The cops won't be looking for it. I did it for you, Jane."

She smiled at him. "For me?"

He nodded. "We'll go to a safe place. We'll travel...see the world...spend lots of money."

Her eyes gleamed. "You promise? You have to promise me, Michael."

"You bet. I have a generous trust fund. Remember?"

"Which fund? The one your grandmother set up? Or your parents?"

"Both. Millions of dollars just sitting there. What do you say? Want to help me spend it?"

"Definitely." Jane laughed. "I knew you'd see it my way." She lowered the gun but kept it aimed in my direction. "We should get rid of her."

"Forget it. She can't even move. She's done. It won't be long now." He waved her toward him. "Come on. Let's go, Jane. We have better things to do." He headed for the door.

She hesitated, then said, "You're right." She turned off the lights, grabbed her overnight bag by the door, and followed him out.

"Michael!" My voice was hoarse. "Help me!"

He had left me here to die. This couldn't be happening. He was supposed to protect me.

Maybe this was another hallucination, another of my wild illusions. There was no other explanation.

I was so tired. Tired of fighting. Tired of not knowing if I were imagining things or not. I closed my eyes and drifted away, conceding that the gray blobs would suck me up once and for all.

∾

The floor beneath me vibrated.

Heavy footsteps approached.

I opened my eyes.

Beams of light sliced through the darkness.

Had they put me back in the closet?

No! Not again!

I covered my eyes and prepared for the thumping of loud music to start up. But it didn't.

I peeked through my fingers.

Shadows stood over me. No, wait. Not shadows. Two uniformed officers.

One officer bent over me and spoke into his radio microphone. "Victim Megan Scott located!"

I was safe! I broke into tears and shook uncontrollably as someone wrapped a blanket around me.

But what about Michael? Where was he?

37

MICHAEL

Saturday night

Although Michael cautiously steered the car along the dimly lit Morin Road, he remained acutely aware of the woman sitting beside him. He'd gotten lucky when he persuaded Jane to leave her SUV at the cabin and hop into his leased car instead—one that the cops wouldn't be looking for.

Two QPP cruisers, an unmarked car, and a SWAT vehicle whizzed by in the opposite lane. He was certain they were headed for the cabin. His tactic to save Megan had worked.

Jane noticed the vehicles too. "Did you see that? Those fools! They're going the wrong way." She laughed.

Michael forced a chuckle. "Yeah."

"You were right to take your car and not my SUV. I knew I could trust you." She touched his cheek.

He stiffened but managed a brief smile. He wanted to believe that the cops would reach Megan in time, that medics would be on hand to treat her. If only help had arrived earlier so he could have stayed with Megan and avoided this next phase with Jane, but it wasn't meant to be.

Jane's perceived triumph over Megan had obscured the wary scrutiny she usually exercised. It was what Michael had counted on. He'd encouraged her fantasies, taken her hand as they left the cabin, and then graciously opened the door for her on the passenger side. He'd smiled at her as he slid in behind the wheel, all the while knowing that the driver's seat gave him the ultimate control over their destination.

Megan.

He'd left her behind so brutally, all alone and in such rough shape. He had no choice but to string Jane along. Megan had to understand that he'd never leave her for the likes of Jane or any other woman. But would she be able to understand that he was merely playing a game—though a deadly one at that?

He glanced at Jane. Moonlight danced over an expression of self-satisfaction mixed with excitement, highlighting the wild workings of her mind. She turned to him with a smile and a wink, as if she'd won a victory of sorts, then reached over to squeeze his hand. Her touch disgusted him, but he squeezed back. He had to continue to play the game.

Rusty Homer had been right in his assessment of the most likely suspect. It was Jane who had the most to gain. Unlike the other suspects on Michael's list who wanted revenge against him, Jane directed her vengeance against Megan but schemed to keep him for herself. A win-win situation for her.

Megan.

He'd noticed her lethargic state, the vacant look in her eyes, the weight she'd lost. Gone was the usual spark of responsiveness or even awareness of his presence beside her. If she hadn't been able to process what was happening, she couldn't possibly have seen through his fake escapade with Jane.

He was familiar with the psychological torture techniques that adversaries use to break down prisoners and get them to talk. Jane was obviously acquainted with them too, and she'd capitalized on that knowledge.

He'd encountered hardcore abusers—including a couple of

women—during investigative stints. Not many had come close to exhibiting the intense level of revenge that Jane had inflicted on Megan, not to mention how easily she'd shot Lardo. He shuddered to think that he was sitting inches away from her.

Megan had screamed out for him as he was leaving the cabin with Jane. It had torn him apart. In her neglected and brainwashed condition, maybe she couldn't decipher what was real and what wasn't. She could have imagined all sorts of things. It didn't change anything, though. Her desperate plea to him was horribly real, and it kept running through his mind.

All the same, he was positive he'd made the right move in leaving Megan behind. He wouldn't have been able to forgive himself if Jane had shot her. But while logic dictated that he'd made a justifiable decision, his conscience was still beating him up. He'd abandoned her.

Hang on, Megan. Please hang on.

Michael had luck on his side so far. That he'd managed to get Jane to walk away and spare Megan's life was a feat in itself. That destiny would grant him a similar fate had yet to be determined. He didn't know how long he could carry on this charade with Jane. Since her thoughts fluctuated from sane to irrational the way they did when she wasn't on medication, he feared she might soon recognize his ruse for the sham it was.

He conceded that he might have to contend with Jane on his own. Even kill her, if he had to defend himself. He couldn't phone for help and ask for backup from the cops. Not with Jane breathing down his neck.

What disturbed him the most was that she'd brought along her father's shotgun. Did she doubt the validity of his words?

He'd have to come up with more strategies to convince her that his intentions were sincere, or else she'd get rid of him too. Her trust in him had caused her to ignore a vital factor until now: They were heading back to Montreal.

Jane said, "You're quiet all of a sudden."

"I'm thinking about the future," he said, improvising. "Our future."

"Oh. So where are we going, Michael?"

For a second, he assumed she'd snapped back to a more realistic state of mind. "Wherever you want," he said, winging it again.

"As long as I'm with you, that's all that matters." She put a hand on his arm.

He hated her touch, the way her eyes lingered on him, her mere presence next to him. He concealed his revulsion with a grin and said, "Let's head back to Montreal. The cops won't expect us to return there. We can take the next plane out. What do you say?"

She frowned. "No, it's not safe. They'll be looking for me at the airport. Besides, I don't have a passport."

Just what he needed. Another glitch.

They would reach the exit to the main highway soon. He had to convince her that Montreal was the most viable option. If he failed, she might urge him to drive deeper into the woodlands of Quebec instead.

Jane's face lit up in the next instant. "I have an idea. Let's take a train from Montreal to Toronto instead. I have cash, so we don't need to use credit. We can take a flight out of Toronto. How about it?"

Michael perceived vehicles blocking the road ahead. A police barrier? Yes!

To distract Jane, he pumped a fist in the air. "Let's go for it!"

She laughed. "That's the spirit." She peered through the windshield. "Is that a police blockade?"

Several squad cars had lined up with a SWAT truck to form a barricade across the road. As Michael neared, he opened the window on the driver's side and flashed his headlights.

"What are you doing?" Jane shrieked. "Turn around! Now!"

He hit the brakes and cut the ignition, then hurled the keys out the window. "No, Jane. We're done."

Her eyes widened. "You can't be serious."

"I'm deadly serious."

"You can't do this to me—to us, Michael. You promised that we—"

"I lied."

"No!" Jane lunged at Michael, striking him on the head. "You hypocrite! I trusted you."

He grabbed her arms, thrusting her away, pinning her to the passenger door. "I said we're done."

She didn't fight him off. "You have no idea how fantastic it would have been between us." She smiled, her voice softening. "We would have made such a terrific couple."

Michael felt her body slacken but maintained his grasp on her arms. "Don't you get it? Megan and I are a couple. That'll never change."

Her tone turned frosty. "She must be dead by now."

"It wouldn't change a thing." He gritted his teeth. "Your plan was a failure from the start."

Rage swept over her. "You're saying that I did all this for nothing?"

"You got it." He broke his hold on her.

"Damn you!" Jane snarled and reached for the shotgun on the back seat.

Michael grabbed it and struggled to break her hold on it. He was amazed at her strength and how hard she fought. As he wrestled the shotgun out of her hands, he accidentally hit her in the forehead with the butt.

Dazed, Jane let go of the gun and reeled back against the passenger window.

Michael tossed the shotgun onto the road and stepped out, hands above his head. He left the door ajar and slowly moved away from the car.

"Don't shoot! It's Michael Elliott!" a familiar male voice boomed from the shadows behind the police blockade.

Esposito!

Michael shifted his view to Jane. The overhead light in the car revealed a blank expression on her face. What was she planning now?

A police command crackled through the loudspeaker. "Jane Barlow, come out with your hands over your head!"

Jane didn't move.

Another police command broke through the air. "Come out with your hands over your head *now!*"

Jane rushed out, circled the rear of the car, and seized the shotgun. She stood facing the blockade, her shotgun slightly raised.

SWAT members fixed their weapons on her.

"Put down your gun!" an officer ordered.

Jane fixed her gaze on Michael. "You know, I always loved you." She smiled at him.

Michael bristled. It was the same creepy smile that she'd given him when they'd taken her away to jail in handcuffs years earlier.

Jane aimed her shotgun at the officers and fired. She kept on shooting, cursing at them all the while.

Officers shot back.

Jane collapsed to the ground.

It was over.

38

MICHAEL

Weeks later

Michael visited Megan every day during her stay in the hospital. The trauma she'd endured had taken its toll on her. She was pale, had lost weight, and was often confused. Seeing her so weak and vulnerable pained him.

Her physical health improved steadily after her return home, thanks in large part to her mother's frequent visits and the nutritious meals she prepared. Michael was relieved to see Megan up and around again. Her life was back on track.

Or was it?

The consequences of the psychological agony Megan had suffered told a different story. Terrifying nightmares about Jane often woke her up in a panic. At times, she seemed to live in a world of her own. She was her old sassy self one moment, only to slide back into a silent, wistful state the next. He feared she was dwelling too much on the past. As was he.

Their therapy sessions with Dr. Katherine Madison helped him to understand the guilt he still shouldered about the kidnapping. He'd abandoned Megan when she needed him the most. How could he ever forget?

Then there was Jane. Could he have predicted that she'd provoke the cops into killing her? Was it her way of redeeming herself? Making amends? Or was it a final tactic to make him feel guilty for the rest of his life?

He had to let it go. He would never be able to understand, nor did he especially want to.

As for Megan, the healing process would take time. What she'd suffered could have long-term effects, Dr. Madison said. She suggested that they focus on other things, rather than dwell on the past.

They followed her advice. Michael went back to his job. Megan took on minor ghostwriting contracts. He grew hopeful. She was finally putting the past behind her.

Then a setback. Exhaustion drained Megan after only a few hours of work. She had difficulty concentrating and slept a lot. The shrink said sleep was her way of healing. Michael had no problem with that.

He did, however, have another personal problem to resolve: his relationship with his father. Days after he'd notified his parents that Megan had been rescued, he called his father back. "Dad, we need to talk."

"Is everything okay with Megan?" his father asked.

"Yes, yes. What I'm calling about is..." He paused. "I want to explain why I've kept you and Mom at a distance for so long."

"Oh?"

"Since you and I haven't been on the best of terms, I didn't think it was fair to expose Megan to the friction between us. I'm sorry I did that."

There was an awkward moment of silence.

His father spoke. "I'm the one who should be apologizing. I was selfish when I expected you to take over my company, and my pride was hurt when you refused. I can see now that your career is the right one for you—and a timely one at that. If you

wouldn't have been there for Megan when it mattered most..."
His voice trailed off.

Michael gulped. It was the first time his father had been so
candid about his feelings. "Did Mom persuade you to call—"

"No, she didn't. The risks you took to save Megan's life made
me realize how brave you are. The ethical duties you take on as
investigative reporter are beyond reproach. I'm so proud of you,
son. Will you ever forgive me for doubting you?"

Michael had experienced a roller coaster of emotions lately,
but his father's words offered a pinnacle of hope for a closer
relationship between them. "It's all good. Thanks, Dad."

In the weeks that followed, Michael kept up to date with the
police investigation into Megan's kidnapping. Because of Ken
Reilly's cooperation in tracking down Tiny, the cops suspended
charges against him for selling illegal drugs. In return, Ken
would spend two hundred hours doing community service
work.

Gabe Rivard's punishment was more telling. He'd survived
his plunge into a ravine and escaped death, only to be
sentenced to ten years in jail for attempted murder. Michael
knew it wasn't over by a long shot. He'd continue to be fair
game upon Rivard's release. Or maybe sooner, depending on
the guy's influence on other members of the Hells Angels.

On a side note, the cops searched the blue sedan that Rivard
had driven the night of the accident. They found bags of
fentanyl pills with a market value of a million dollars hidden in
the compartments behind the back seats. Talk about a fluke!
They traced the stash to an illegal drug-trafficking operation in
Sainte-Adèle and arrested members of the Hells Angels.

Michael smiled. Willie's tipoff had struck pay dirt again.

The cops discovered another stash of a different sort in the
basement of the Parkvale Street house. A plastic bag tucked

behind the TV held a thousand dollars in twenty-dollar bills. It came with a note that read: *For my little brother, Nat.*

When Michael told Megan about it, she said it was probably the money that Jane had given Lardo. She believed he'd left it behind on purpose.

Michael wasn't surprised when the cops charged Darcy Barlow with aiding and abetting a criminal. Although the man claimed he knew nothing about Megan's kidnapping, he'd given Jane money after she escaped from jail and made his cabin available to her.

Michael noted Darcy Barlow's trial date in his agenda. He'd be there.

39

———

MEGAN

Weeks later

"Let me out!" I pounded my fists against the door.

The walls of the tiny closet were closing in on me. I had difficulty breathing. I was suffocating!

The door swung open and Jane sneered at me. Tall flames roared up behind her. "You didn't think I'd leave you here, did you?" She grabbed my arm and yanked me out.

I tried to pull away, but my legs stiffened. I couldn't move.

"Welcome home," she said, smirking, as she dragged me toward the fires of hell.

The flames grew hotter and hotter. I couldn't breathe.

No! No!

I jerked up in bed, my neck drenched in sweat. I gulped a breath of air, then another. It was okay. I was home. I was safe.

In the initial and darker days after my rescue, I'd had the same recurring nightmare—except for nights when flashbacks of the pain and terror I'd endured prevented me from sleeping at all. Michael would wrap his arms around me and whisper how much he loved me and that he'd always protect me.

Dr. Katherine Madison, my psychologist, explained that I was subconsciously punishing myself for having fallen into Jane's trap. Maybe she was right.

I struggled to get through those turbulent days when Jane infiltrated my thoughts and haunted my dreams. I eventually accepted that she was dead and wouldn't return. No longer would I need to dread that she was stalking me or planning to kill me. She was gone.

But I wasn't free from the mental anguish of the ordeal.

And neither was Michael.

Our joint battle with Jane had led to consultations with Dr. Madison to help alleviate the trauma we'd experienced. Michael was trying to banish unwarranted guilty feelings for having left me in the cabin alone. I was practicing meditation techniques to overcome panic attacks every time I opened a closet door. We agreed to continue our therapy sessions for as long as the doctor considered them necessary.

The hearing loss that I'd suffered from the loud music was reversible and would gradually return to normal. It was comforting to hear Michael's deep voice and calm words clearly once more, such that he'd often read to me at night as part of my sleep therapy.

Oh, I had no problem falling asleep. I did a lot of that. The nightmares that woke me up were the problem.

Although I'd lost bits of memory from my confinement time in the cabin closet, Michael believed it was all for the better. He promised we'd create new memories to replace them.

But I had my doubts. I was still wrestling to suppress ugly memories of Jane that surfaced unpredictably like clips from a horror movie.

Michael, however, was determined to fulfill his promise. He came home one evening with a lovely painting of us and hung it on a wall in the living room. Enrico had painted it from a photo Michael had provided.

"You really like it?" he asked me.

I smiled. "I love it."

I sometimes worried that Michael would raise the subject of house hunting again, but he didn't. That's what I loved about him. He understood me best. And because of it, I trusted him.

Michael returned to his job at *The Gazette* two weeks after my rescue. He said he wanted to bring normalcy back to his daily routine. I was okay with that. My guess was that he was bored to death babysitting me.

I wasn't bored. I had a lot on my mind, such that the hours floated by like snowflakes on a windless winter day, and I would lose track of time. Michael would occasionally pop in at lunch to find me in the same spot he'd left me earlier.

On Dr. Madison's suggestion, I accepted minor projects from Bradford Publishing. I tried but could only manage two hours of work every day. My concentration wasn't what it used to be. According to the doctor, the psychological consequences of my trauma would take a lot more time to heal.

Family support sped up my recuperation. My mother visited often and cooked my favorite meals in our kitchen while I watched. I was still her little girl, she said, in spite of my protests otherwise. In truth, I valued her presence more than ever.

Michael surprised me when he suggested we invite my mother and his parents to dinner one weekend. He said he had smoothed things out with his father. That fact alone raised my spirits, and I looked forward to the event.

His parents hugged Michael and me tightly on their arrival. Their genuine affection assured me that they had our welfare at heart, as did their encouraging words.

I was standing beside Michael when he whispered to his father, "Thanks for believing in me, Dad."

His father smiled and patted him on the back. "I'm glad we had that talk."

Trust is earned, never given. Michael's words echoed in my mind.

The cheerful vibes continued as we sat down at the dinner table and enjoyed my mother's homemade lasagna. It was the first time in weeks that I remained focused on the conversation, and my mood didn't slip to a gloomier side. There was hope for me after all.

After we served coffee, Michael's mother said to me, "I can tell by the way you and Michael look at each other that you share something special."

I smiled at her, then reached over and squeezed Michael's hand. "We do."

"Michael is a real hero," my mother said, her expression beaming with pride. "I'm grateful to have such a brave man in my daughter's life."

"I promise I'll always be there for her." Michael slipped a protective arm around me. "I love her."

My mother reached for her glass of wine. "To love, then."

Glasses clinked and wishes of good health and friendship flowed.

"Megan, we'd like to invite you, Michael, and your mother for a visit to our home in the country. We have six bedrooms and lots of land with trails and meadows."

Wide-open spaces. Exactly what I needed. "Sounds like an excellent plan."

ACKNOWLEDGMENTS

The completion of *Cold Revenge* was due to a collective effort of devoted and talented people. My gratitude goes out to the beta readers, proofreaders, editor, and cover designer who contributed valuable feedback to the process and made my work shine.

I also want to thank my family and friends for their patience and encouragement. I wouldn't have made it this far without you.

A special thanks to readers who motivate me to keep on writing. I'm so grateful for your kind comments and continued interest in my work.

ABOUT THE AUTHOR

Sandra Nikolai is the author of the Megan Scott/Michael Elliott Mystery series. In addition to her novels, Sandra has published a string of short crime stories, garnering awards along the way.

A graduate of McGill University in Montreal, Sandra held jobs in sales, finance, and high tech before leaving the corporate world to pursue a career in writing. She likes to think that plotting a whodunit reveals the lighter—yet more mysterious—side of her persona.

Visit www.sandranikolai.com and sign up for Sandra's quarterly newsletter to get news on book releases, exclusive promotions, and other inside information. Your email address will never be shared and you can unsubscribe at any time.

You can also find Sandra on Twitter or connect with her on Facebook and Instagram at SandraNikolaiAuthor.

ALSO BY SANDRA NIKOLAI

Megan Scott/Michael Elliott Mystery series on Amazon:

False Impressions

Fatal Whispers

Icy Silence

Dark Deeds

Broken Trust